"Chandler is a first-rate wordsmith..."
THE DENVER POST

"Jon Chandler's bond with the cowboy way is an extension
of his heritage... the straight ahead, no-nonsense clarity of
his writing shoots almost like hot lead to the very heart of
the cowboy experience."
PAUL PAPE, TRAIL DUST MAGAZINE

The
SPANISH
PEAKS

First Edition 1998
Second Printing June 1999
Third Printing December 2000

Printed in the United States of America

The Spanish Peaks is published by:

Rodgers & Nelsen Publishing Co.
P. O. Box 7001
Loveland, CO 80537-0001
970/593-9557

Production Credits:

Edited by Barbara Teel
Cover Design by Kenn Hayes
Illustrations by Beverly J. Nelsen
Cover Photo by Gordon Kelley
Electronic Prepress by Teel & Co.

ISBN 0-9662696-0-8

The
SPANISH
PEAKS

A NOVEL OF FRONTIER COLORADO

by
Jon Chandler

Rodgers & Nelsen
Publishing Co

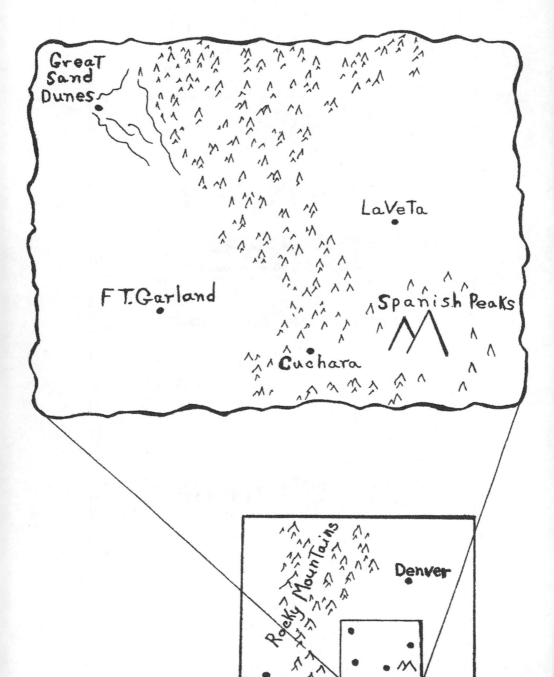

EPIGRAPH

Filipio Garcia seemed on edge and quickly strode to a tree where he had leaned his rifle. He picked it up and checked it, then returned it to its spot before walking a few yards to pick up his gunbelt. Awkwardly attempting to strap the belt around his waist, he cursed as he fumbled with the buckle, unable to fully use his left hand to hold it steady. He finally slipped the belt through the buckle and latched it, then turned back to retrieve the rifle.

A man stood next to it, pointing a huge buffalo rifle directly at Garcia's midsection. Half his body was behind the tree, offering a small target. Dressed in stained buckskins and a low-crowned felt hat, he seemed to be an Indian. Stunned, the outlaw could do nothing but work his jaw back and forth, desperately trying to overcome the shock and regain his senses.

"Seems like yeer pardner's gone and stole yer hosses," said the man flatly, and suddenly Filipio Garcia knew.

Regaining his voice, he said in rough, accented English, "So, it is true. You are a ghost."

Tate did not answer, but briefly checked the outlaw over. With a sneer, he said, "Naw, I ain't no ghost. But yee're about to be."

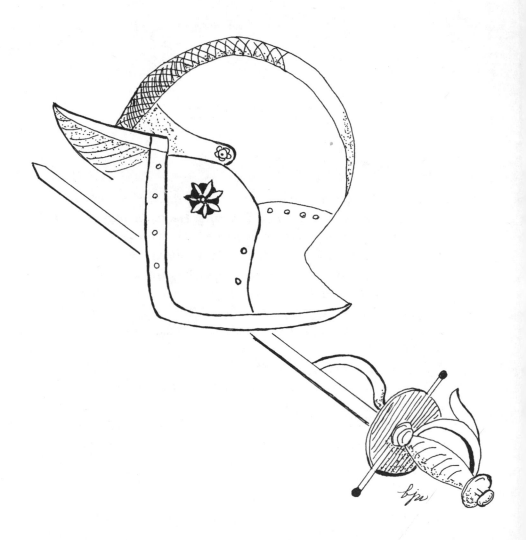

*"He wore the armor... to impress
and intimidate the savages..."*

PROLOGUE

New Spain, 1541

CAPTAIN DON FRANCISCO ALVARADO removed the sweltering
metal helmet encasing his head and ran his hand through
his sweat-soaked hair. Although there was a slight chill in
the air, he was burning up with fever. Luckily, a cool breeze
stirred from the mountains above and served to refresh
him. At least he felt he would not fall from the high-backed
saddle he occupied astride an impressive stallion.

He wore the armor, he supposed, to impress and intimidate the savages who guided him north, but now that the
last of them had run off, there was little need. He turned
and lashed the helmet to the rear of the saddle and with-
drew from a pouch a red woolen cap, which he quickly
pulled down over his fair hair.

Although his breath was labored, he still could not help
but stare in awe at the country surrounding him. The sky
was the brightest of blues, descending to meet the lofty
peaks on either side. A seemingly never ending forest of
pine and aspen extended up the middle of a broad saddle
of land, covering the slopes to the north and south.

He traveled this way out of both necessity and desperation. He had been told by savages days ago that this was a
pass through the mountains, and that once over it he

3

would be able to travel south through the forsaken lands to Spanish settlements. But with each passing moment, he realized that his situation grew more and more precarious.

He was ill. Very ill. It had begun several weeks before when he left Coronado's command with orders to search for gold near two twin peaks to the north. The peaks had been described to the Spanish commander by savages as being a place where gold literally ran down the streams. They were called, he was told, the Wa-ha-to-ya. The mystified Coronado asked his interpreter what the name signified. After a brief discussion, he was told the Wa-ha-to-ya were considered by the savages to be the breasts of the world. Coronado had wryly considered the context of the name, and immediately made a decision. *Huajatolla they shall remain, then,* he had said.

Coronado assembled a party consisting of Alvarado, Mendoza and Escobel, and ordered them to travel to the *Huajatolla* with several newly baptized savages, who were also guides. The priest Santos was also dispatched.

Striking out north from the Spanish encampment, the group traveled through vast stretches of desert, finally sighting the twin peaks after nearly two weeks. By this time, Escobel had been coughing for days, and had developed a raging fever.

They continued their journey, and within two days were encamped on the northeastern side of the *Huajatolla*. Alvarado had been amazed. The peaks rose straight up from the flat, dusty plain before connecting to the range of giant mountains to the west. He thought how aptly they were named.

That night, Escobel coughed up great amounts of blood, and by the next morning was dead. Ground was consecrated near a magnificent cottonwood tree, and the Spaniard was hastily buried.

Alvarado and Mendoza spent much time with the savages, having them draw maps. They learned of a large river two days to the north, and of a pass to the west of *Huajatolla* that would provide easier access to the new Spanish provinces.

Over the ensuing days, three savages developed identical symptoms to those of Escobel and finally died in the same horrific manner. Even though Father Santos prayed over them, they still died, and the remaining savages slipped out of the encampment. The next morning, the priest knelt praying for the souls of Christ's savages. As if a magic trick, six arrows suddenly and silently protruded from his body.

Alvarado and Mendoza decided to try to make it back to Coronado's party. Mendoza would follow the same route they had taken, while Alvarado would try the pass to the west, in hope of finding another route to access the northern mountains.

He began to feel uneasy as he ascended the sloping foothills. His throat burned, and he was gasping for breath.

The next day, he was worse, yet he donned his armor in case he would run into savages. Now, in the thin air of the high mountains, he was near exhaustion.

Riding further, he felt himself slipping from the saddle and with great effort barely freed his feet from the carved wooden stirrups. He crashed to the ground, landing on his side, bruising his ribs against the thin metal of his armored breastplate. His horse merely stood and looked down at him, as if ridiculing him for his weakness. With monumental effort, he stood on unsteady legs and grabbed onto the saddle to stabilize himself.

Although dizzy and weak, he surveyed the surrounding area, hoping to find shelter. Several yards away, tucked into the side of a hill was a stone outcropping, its inset mica sparkling in the sunlight. Below the outcropping was what appeared to be a fairly deep hole. A gnarled evergreen grew to one side, partially obscuring the entrance. Alvarado staggered toward the entry and stuck his head

5

inside. As his eyes adjusted, he saw that it was large enough to provide shelter, so he painfully dragged himself back to his horse and removed his weapons and valuables. His sword was largely ceremonial, but could be used effectively in a confrontation. The musket, of course, was an implement of destruction that gave the Spanish superiority over the savage hordes. And his knife, actually a keen, double-edged, foot-long dagger of forged steel with an ornamental brass handle, was both useful and deadly. Lastly, he grabbed his armored helmet, thinking it might be useful to frighten any savages who might find him.

He slowly carried the armor and weapons into the depression, then unsteadily returned to the stallion. He wrapped its reins around a tree branch but failed to notice when it pulled away and began heading east as Alvarado lurched toward the entrance to the shelter.

Once inside, he collapsed into a fitful sleep. When he awoke, he realized with finality that he was going to die here in this foreign, godless land. He finally managed to prop his head up on the helmet and opened his eyes to view the landscape outside the small cave. Across the valley, groves of quaking aspen seemed to make the mountainside move, and Alvarado thought he had never seen anything as beautiful. He thought of his home in Castile, of his beautiful wife Therese, and their two boys. They would never know what happened, he thought sadly. But then they would never know the beauty of this, his final resting place.

A bright shaft of sunlight suddenly pierced the depression as the sun lowered in the western sky. As it bathed his face in brilliance, he began to pray aloud, tears streaming down his cheeks. An hour later, his voice was still.

In memory of my grandfather,
Russell Patterson, "Bop," who told me the stories.

*"...Herold's Crossing was no longer
just a piece of hard, nearly uninhabitable
ground—it was their home."*

CHAPTER ONE

JAKE HEROLD STOOD in the doorway of the trading post that had, over the years, assumed his name. A man used to backbreaking labor, Jake seemed totally at ease as he slapped the dust from his low-crowned hat and jammed it on his head. He squinted his eyes in the bright noonday sun and continued to look toward the horizon.

His calm demeanor belied the racing of his heart as he made his decision, reached inside the building and, with one swift motion, lifted and cocked the double-barreled shotgun.

His gaze was riveted on the three riders approaching from the southeast at a quick gallop. For the past minute, he had watched the tiny riders grow ever larger until he realized they were not men of the *Cucharas.* They were in a hurry, and in the foothills country of southern Colorado, speed generally meant trouble.

The ramshackle collection of split-pine buildings known as Herold's Crossing had become an important trade center to the people of the lower Cucharas Valley, providing respite for travelers and supplies for the locals. Had Herold been a less headstrong man, it also might have made easy pickings for the *bandidos* and outlaws who frequented the nearby Santa Fe Trail. In the early years, some had tried. The small graveyard a mile up Crow Hill attested to their failures. Herold was, of necessity, a careful man.

As the riders approached, he glanced at the sky behind them and noticed that the plume of smoke he'd been watching for the past hour had begun to dissipate. The fire, most likely at the Gorner or Fontineau spreads, must have either burned out or been put out. He wondered what these riders had to do with it.

"John. Stephen. Grab your arms!" he yelled.

His two sons looked up from their work, dropped the rigging they were repairing, and came running from the north side of the pine building. John, a sandy-haired brick of a boy who at 15 already exhibited the exceptional strength of his father, took up a Henry rifle that had been covered by an oil soaked tarp in the back of a wagon. Stephen, the smaller of the two although older by two years, disappeared into the barn and came running back out, hurriedly strapping on the belt that holstered his father's Navy Colt.

Herold pointed toward the corner of the porch, behind a stack of nail kegs.

"Johnny, set up there.

"Steve, you take cover behind the livery door."

While Stephen raced to the adjacent building, Herold turned quietly, finding Libby and Amos standing at his side.

"Lib, I don't know what we got here. Trouble, most likely," he said.

Her eyes showed the same determination he'd seen 18 years before when they'd arrived at this crossing of the Cucharas River. These days, however, her resolve was tempered by the years, their three sons, and the fact that Herold's Crossing was no longer just a piece of hard, nearly uninhabitable ground—it was their home.

She touched Amos, who had just turned thirteen, on the

shoulder and they disappeared inside the tiny store.

The riders spread out as they approached, a preventative and nearly automatic action throughout the West that served to provide scattered targets for enemy fire.

Herold scanned the three riders as they slowed their advance. He recognized them from the descriptions spread by lawmen and soldiers. He'd been right. Trouble.

"Garcias," he whispered to himself.

The center and far left riders slowed their lathered horses while the rider to the right circled outward toward the compound's corrals. All wore filthy *serapes,* covered with trail dust and grease. The gray broadcloth pants of the center rider were ripped above the right knee and soaked with blood. Caked blood also coated his dun horse's right rear flank. Flies swarmed around the blood, causing the horse to continually switch its tail to brush the wound.

Two riders sported several days' growth of beard and full, grimy moustaches. The other was but a boy, a few light hairs sprouting above his upper lip. One rider was hatless while the other two wore the broadbrimmed hats favored by the *vaqueros* to the south. They were obviously kin.

Herold strode purposefully to the front of the porch as the riders to either side stopped, and the center rider entered the large clearing that stretched out before the compound.

Herold held the shotgun loosely in the crook of his elbow, his right index finger poised on the forward trigger. He stared directly into the eyes of the man who stopped twenty yards away.

"We need food. Medicine," said the rider in a thick Spanish accent. He sat erect in the saddle, controlling the pain his wounded leg must have caused him.

Herold continued to stare at him. Then his eyes fell to the wounded horse and a sheathed rifle attached to a newly-made saddle.

A tic began in the muscles of his cheek as he refocused

his steely glare with incredible intensity, and watched the rider carefully rub his unshaven jaw in reaction. Finally, he slowly said, "Gorner's. You been to the Gorner's."

"Eh?" said the rider, confused and wary.

"You're sittin' on Jed Gorner's saddle and carryin' his rifle. And from the look of your leg and your horse's rump, you ran through some wire he strung up a coupla weeks ago—trying to keep his cattle penned up. Only people in these parts with wire are the Gorners."

The horseman looked nervously around to ensure his companions were spread out behind him. His shifty eyes took in the scene, calculating, adjusting to various distances.

"I know nothing about Gorners or wire," he finally said. "We need supplies and medicine. You will sell to us. We will pay."

"I don't accept blood money from murderin' thieves, *Garcia*."

The rider's dark eyes momentarily opened wide, affirming the identification. He controlled his surprise and offered Herold only a flat stare in reply.

"Oh, yeah, word travels. Las Cruces, Santa Fe, even Canon City. You boys cut a wider swath than most the past coupla years. There's talk that the Gov'nor finally put a bounty on your heads."

Garcia's glittering black eyes were blazing.

"You will sell us supplies, or we will take them," he sneered.

Herold nearly chuckled at the outlaw's bravado. It was time to end the game.

"Nah. You won't."

The rider shifted the reins to his left hand and pulled the serape up over the saddle's pommel, exposing a holstered Colt. His hand went slowly past the pistol and expertly pulled a leather thong from over the butt of the sheathed rifle.

Herold's shotgun had imperceptibly moved up and was pointed directly at the rider's chest.

"Try it, and there'll be pieces of you hanging from the willows yonder."

The dark rider smiled as his hand pulled back from the rifle.

"I, too know things. Jake Herold is a dangerous *hombre,* it is said. Yet, I find only a man who talks of *wire* and boys," he smirked. "Interesting."

He sat silently for a few moments. The dun snorted and reared its head a couple of times, and finally pawed the ground.

The outlaw seemed to make a decision. Herold noticed a quick hand signal. The other adult rider, situated to the right, suddenly pulled back his serape, palmed his pistol and fired twice in the general direction of Stephen, entrenched behind the livery door.

Herold's shotgun instinctively switched to the second rider, his finger tightening on the shotgun's trigger. At that movement, the man before him quickly whipped his rifle from its scabbard. With lightning speed he cocked the repeater and was leveling it at Herold when the window of the trading post exploded outward. Shattered glass erupted over the porch. The shot fired from inside the building struck the dark rider in the shoulder, throwing him backward and nearly off his mount. He screamed in agony as his terrified horse leaped skyward, spinning clockwise all the while, and lit out at a full gallop away from the flying glass.

Garcia grabbed for the saddle's pommel with his good arm and allowed his rifle to clatter to the ground as he clung in wild desperation to the rampaging horse. In an instant, the dun was galloping away from the courtyard, out of control. The other riders had already turned their mounts, and followed in a flash. Herold and John dashed into the courtyard, each firing at the fleeing riders, more as an afterthought to the astonishing proceedings than with deadly intent.

Herold, worried about Stephen, turned to the livery in time to see his oldest son holstering the Navy Colt.

"You all right Steve? You hit?"

"I'm fine, Pa," answered Stephen. The boy was shaking with excitement and fear.

"Momma!" he yelled. "You hit him!"

Libby had stepped through the front door onto the porch, her arm circled tightly around young Amos's shoulders. The boy, his auburn hair burnished in the bright sunlight, looked stunned.

"It wasn't me," said Libby in a shaking voice.

It was then they noticed that the woman held no weapon, while the boy gripped a Remington so tightly he might have broken the stock.

"It was Amos," she said, crying from relief and hugging the boy tightly.

"Amos saved you, Jake."

After barricading Libby and Amos inside the trading post—making sure they were well armed—Herold, Stephen and John followed the outlaws' trail to the north. Wary of ambushes, they finally satisfied themselves that the *bandidos* were not looping back to plan some revenge at Herold's Crossing. Occasional splattered drops of blood mixed with horses' hoofprints assured them that the outlaws would surely go to ground and not bother anyone for a while. Amos's ability to handle a rifle at his young age had paid off.

Cutting across the rolling prairie of sage, cholla and pinon pine to the Fontineau's ranch, they found Phillip and Marie Fontineau down with fever and unable to have checked on the fire earlier in the day.

Later, as they approached the Gorner spread, they saw a

patch of dun-colored horsehair hanging from the rough baling wire that fenced a small pasture. Partially dried blood glimmered on the twisted wire. Two fence posts were snapped, suspended by the wire perpendicular to the ground. Blood, either man's or horse's, was smeared on one of the posts.

They found Jed's bullet-riddled body lying face up at the edge of his corral. Ten-year-old John Gorner was sprawled in a patch of thistles fifty feet away, shot twice in the back while attempting to run toward safety in a nearby grove of cottonwoods.

Herold anxiously took in the horrific scene, hoping against hope that other, perhaps worse atrocities would not be found. He calmed his sons and had them wait with the bodies while he scouted the still smoldering house. The fire had burned hot, and he was unable to distinguish anything.

Entering the outbuilding that housed the tack, he dropped to one knee, stunned at the sight before him. He found Emily Gorner, her blue gingham dress ripped and torn to shreds, her body horribly violated—her grimace in death dreadful to behold.

Controlling himself with great effort, Herold slowly moved to Emily, gently closed her eyes and covered her body with an old blanket hanging from the tack house wall. He knelt down over the still form and, for the first time in years, wept from frustration and despair.

"We'll get 'em, Emily," he whispered through clenched teeth. "Somehow, I promise we'll get 'em."

The man and his shocked and disconsolate sons carried the bodies of their neighbors—their friends—into the tack shed, closed it securely and rode the twelve miles to Francisco's Fort.

Herold, still shaken, sent his sons to spread word of the day's events to the Fort's shopkeepers while he resolutely walked up to the patioed adobe house on the north side

15

of the square. He knocked on the thick plank door and was admitted by a middle-aged woman.

"I have bad news, *Señora,*" said Herold. "I must speak to *Señor* Francisco."

The woman led him into a spacious parlor, then disappeared behind a woven rug acting as a curtain that separated two rooms. He heard her softly talking, and a masculine voice answering in return.

The rug across the doorway was pulled aside and the legendary pioneer stepped into the living area. Herold was struck for the hundredth time by the man's presence. Although a man of the East, from Portuguese stock, he had assimilated the West, taking it as his own. Living the life of a mountain man and explorer, he had traversed southern Colorado countless times. He fought and made peace with the Ute and Kiowa. He learned the ways of the Mexican settlers and proud old Spanish families. He befriended the early French pioneers, forming a lifelong bond with the legendary mountain man, Ceran St. Vrain. Indeed, Francisco was a legend himself.

Herold knew these days Francisco spoke Spanish as much as English, and was prepared as the pioneer approached him. Francisco's wiry form was held stiffly erect, and his freshly-shaved face, along with his brilliant shock of white hair, gave evidence to a life of adventure and moral certainty.

The old mountain man grasped Herold's outstretched hand. Speaking in formal English, he said, "Jake, you are troubled. What has happened?"

Herold was equally formal. "John, my friend. Vivian Garcia and his band have killed Jed and Emily Gorner and their son. They tried to do the same to me and my family."

"*Aye.* Tell me."

The two men sat in straight-backed chairs and talked for nearly half an hour, forming a plan to deal with the actions necessitated by the murders. Before long, the Herold boys arrived, followed by several men of the settlement. Their demeanor suggested to Herold that they were not a posse but a burial party.

"Jake," said Francisco, "you and your sons return to the Crossing. Libby and the boy should not be left alone. Tomorrow, we will make the hard decisions that must be made. Now, I will send for a man of the cloth to consecrate the ground on the slope above the *Cucharas* where our friends are to be buried.

"Think on what we have discussed today. It is the best way to deal with the Garcias."

Grasping Herold's hand, Francisco softly said, "I'll be ready in the morning when you arrive."

That evening, the Herolds sat before the stone fireplace in the living quarters behind the trading post, bowed their heads as Libby thanked the Lord her God for their deliverance and planned what to do. Their minds, however, were focused on the events of the day.

Following Libby's prayer of deliverance, Herold discussed with his family the basic plan he and Francisco had fleshed out.

"Tomorrow at dawn, I'm going to the *Huajatolla* with John Francisco."

Libby and her three sons looked imploringly at Herold, realizing the difficulty of the mission.

"We're going to find Tate—tell him his daughter and her family have been murdered."

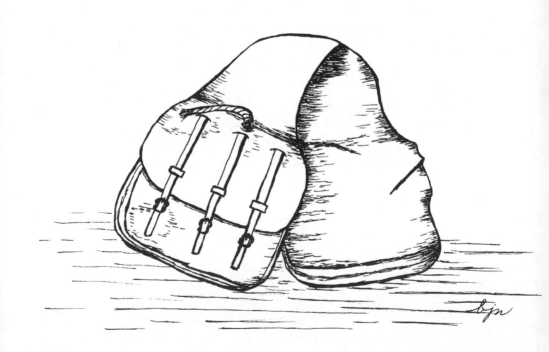

"Finally he returned, bringing with him a remarkable woman..."

CHAPTER TWO

SAM TATE HAD LONG CALLED the Huajatolla the diamond country. It was beautiful, beyond compare in his estimation. Yet, it was also hard, very hard.

Tate had seen only two diamonds in his entire life. One had been worn around the neck of a matron in St. Louis who had hired a nine-year-old Tate to stack firewood. He had, a lifetime ago, stared so intently at the stone that the woman nervously covered it with her hand. Later, when she paid him the few pennies he had earned, he noticed she had removed it.

The other was set in a ring that adorned the buckskin ceremonial shirt of Dog Who Sings, a Crow brave who had taken it from its owner's lifeless hand, along with the finger. The Crow had worn it proudly—it was considered big medicine in the Shining Mountains.

Tate had been fascinated with the stones—by their clarity and brilliance—by their hardened density. Throughout his life he had seen enough glass trading beads to build a palace, yet only diamonds combined both beauty and imperishability, qualities he had admired for over 40 years.

The peculiar connection of the precious stones with

this gorgeous country was more than mere whimsy on his part. He felt the land's sublime spirit, its indestructible character, and viewed it in the manner of the Utes, as a living force.

He had chosen this land as his permanent home for that very reason—he felt it was alive, that he could communicate with it. When he had first seen the Huajatolla—the Spanish Peaks—30 years before on an arduous trek from the Powder River country to the pueblo of Taos, he had sensed the mountains' peculiarities. He had heard of the twin peaks, called *Wa-ha-to-ya* by the Utes—The Breasts of the World. His wonder at them matched what he had felt upon traversing the mighty Tetons.

He found that he wasn't alone in his attraction. The Utes considered the *Wa-ha-to-ya* sacred. Early settlers Duran and Fernandez had carved out homes in the mountains' shadows and had told him stories of their Spanish ancestor's amazement at the majestic peaks, which in the Spanish tongue became *Huajatolla.*

Tate carried their beauty and mystery in the back of his mind through fifteen seasons as a trapper and more as a man of the mountains. Finally, he returned, bringing with him a remarkable woman he had met and married on an infrequent trip back to St. Louis.

The morning sun was reaching over the conifers as Tate took a quick respite. The mountain man had been clearing an area adjacent to his low-roofed cabin. Throughout the morning, over a dozen saplings had fallen to his broad-bladed ax.

He was planning to build a new stable and perhaps a smokehouse. As he aged, his inclination to hunt fresh game, if not his ability, was diminishing. Cattle were at a premium, so a smokehouse seemed in order. Smoked venison, turkey, and the occasional bear would keep him and Esther comfortably fed. Since their daughters were gone, he needed to put up less food, anyway.

Elder daughter Mary had wed William Carson, son of his old *compadre* Kit Carson, and lived over the New Mexico border, at Chama. Their younger daughter Emily had married Jed Gorner, a man determined to bring modern agriculture to the *Huerfano* and *Cucharas* River valleys. Gorner and Tate had grown close, as opposites often do. One was wed to the wind, one to the land. Each understood the other, and each deeply loved Emily. Each also swelled with pride at the mere thought of young John.

With each blow of his ax, Tate was reminded that he was no longer the young buck who set out from St. Louis with a ragtag party of trappers and traders. The years in between had been deadly and dangerous, magical and marvelous.

As a boy he had heard tales of the great men of the frontier—Lewis Wetzel, Daniel Boone, and the outlaws Simon and Jim Girty. He longed for their adventures. Finally, the chance came.

Tate had managed to learn the alphabet and read, despite the illiteracy of his immigrant parents. His father, a rollicking Irishman, was proud of his son's accomplishment, and constantly asked the boy to read to him. With the newspaper as the easiest source, young Tate read aloud to his father, at the same time reveling in the tales of fur trappers that frequently appeared in print. Mountain men, they were called, and their lives of danger and adventure sounded spectacular.

He read of the treacherous assault by the Arikara on Colonel Ashby's party. He learned through a trapper just returned from the West of Tom Fitzpatrick's far-flung discoveries. He even heard of the mountain man Glass's unbelievable crawl to safety following a savage attack by a giant she-bear, a griz it was called.

He was enchanted.

Finally, with his father's blessing, the seventeen-year-old Tate left to explore the West.

21

Joining a trading company, he had followed the Missouri to its source and trapped that first season along the banks of the river Meriwether Lewis had named for Thomas Jefferson. The young man saw wonders of nature that could scarcely be believed. He saw mud boiling in the ground. He smelled the sulphur of Colter's Hell. He stumbled upon a hibernating grizzly during a blinding blizzard, and made use of the old bear's warm shelter until the storm blew itself out.

Over the years, he trapped beaver with Bridger, Beckwourth and Prayin' Jedediah Smith. He fought Blackfeet with Fitzpatrick. He marveled at the drunken squalor of the Green River Rendezvous.

Early on, he spent nearly two seasons with the Snake, learning the intricacies of their dark and moody myths.

He took a Snake wife. He trapped alone, mourning, for over a year after Bright Star's death from the pox.

He learned the ways of the Indians, adopted them, and changed them to fit his white man's sensibilities more readily. As such, most men he chanced to deal with considered him the finest tracker ever to set foot in the Shining Mountains.

At Bent's Fort on the Arkansas River, he met up with a young frontiersman named Christopher "Kit" Carson. He and Kit had formed a friendship that spanned the years, and they were now linked through the union of their children.

He had settled on a life in the shadow of the Spanish Peaks while Kit had followed his ambition. They were separated by a ridge of the Sangre de Cristo mountains, Tate on the east side of La Veta Pass, Carson commanding Fort Garland, an army outpost to the west of the pass at the mouth of a huge valley formed by the Rio Grande River and named for a tiny town, San Luis.

Now, he was a man left to his memories, awaiting the rocking chair with both relish and dread. He was a frontiersman who had, he felt, seen his last frontier.

With senses honed by decades of peril, Tate felt the riders below before he saw them. Even at a great distance, the sun reflecting from white hair belied one rider as Francisco, his old companion. The other he could not yet make out.

Tate laid aside the ax and walked to the house, where Esther would prepare food and drink for their guests.

He entered and looked fondly at his wife of thirty years. Esther Tate sat in a well-worn oak chair, one of the prized possessions she still owned from a long ago and far away life in civilized St. Louis. She was expertly looping spun wool back through itself, accomplishing a tight weave. The blanket was to be a wedding present for Emile Duchette's son and his fiancée, a young girl from Taos.

"Es," said Tate softly, "horsemen comin'. John Francisco and another ridin' a big black, most likely Jake Herold."

Esther quickly stood, put aside the blanket, and hurried toward the back room, where provisions were kept. She stopped, turned and faced Tate.

"It'll be good to see them, Sam," said Esther. "It'll be nice to hear about that Herold family. Those strappin' boys. We should ask Jake and Libby to send one or two on up here, help you with things."

"Whoa, now," Tate said, chuckling. "I got too much time on my hands already."

"That may be so, Sam," she answered, "but swinging an ax is young man's work, just like breakin' trail."

"Well, let's just fill John 'n Jake's gullets a little, an forgit 'bout ax-swingin' young 'uns, shall we?" he said with false gruffness.

"Course, Sam," she said smiling brightly.

Back outside, he continued working until Francisco and Herold rode into the clearing surrounding Tate's home. The mountain man noted their somber bearing.

"Whaugh," he whispered, under his breath. "Somethin'

wrong here."

The two riders slowly approached, Francisco on his tough, sinewy bay pony, Herold on a magnificent black. As they dismounted, Tate noticed the quick stares they gave each other. They were definitely nervous.

"John, Jake. Light and set."

"Sam," said Francisco. "It has been much too long."

"Hello, Sam," said Herold. "Good to see you."

"Same here," said Tate. He gathered the horses' reins, turned and led them to a corral.

Tate had yet to dodge trouble in his life. He did not intend to start now.

"Ye lads're ridin' low in the saddle. Seems like ye got the jitters."

He stared hard at them, then said flatly, "Ye come up here for more than a sociable chat."

Francisco looked at his old friend for a moment, steeling himself for what must be said.

"Yes, Sam. We bring bad news."

Francisco swallowed hard and continued.

"Vivian Garcia and his kin are on the *Cucharas*. They attacked Jake at the Crossing. Jake backtracked and found that they had ambushed and killed Jed."

Francisco paused for a second, and with great difficulty, looked Tate in the eye.

"Emily is dead, Sam."

Tate's even stare concealed his heart's wild pounding, the rising wrath, the immediate and conflicting emotions that called for both disbelief and revenge.

"Whaugh," he half-whispered, his confused mind assessing the information. Then it struck him like a cold spring shower—*John!* What about John?

"The boy?" he said grimly.

"Young John, also," Francisco gently assented.

Tate turned to the forest and stared for nearly a minute. When he turned back, his brown eyes were fixed in a stare of deadly fury. Controlling himself, he turned to Herold.

"Jake, tell this child everythin'."

When Herold had done so, Tate took a deep, shuddering breath and stared at the peaks above. The *Huajatolla* were particularly striking today, the deep green of the pines blending with the bright blues and earth hues at the peaks' summits.

The spirits will try to soothe me today, he thought. *They cannot.*

He made a decision and softly spoke to the men before him.

"John. Jake. This is a hard, hard thing. Yee're pards to carry this burden."

Speaking in Spanish, Tate addressed Francisco. "Ah, Señor Francisco. We have lost many *compañeros* over the years, have we not? This day, though, I have lost my daughter and grandson. I have lost a man whom I respect greatly.

"Whaugh. The Garcias will die hard deaths."

He turned to Herold and, speaking in English, said, "Jake, I am glad your family was not harmed.

"Now, I must tell Esther. God alone kin help me."

The mountain man paused and said kindly to his friends, "Please, ye must go now. We're to be alone with our grief.

"I'll be at yer Fort, John—for supplies. When things are..." he paused, unable for a moment to face the brutal reality, then continued, "done here, I need to git on over to Fort Garland.

"Me'n Kit'll have to figger this thing out."

*"On the west was the gigantic expanse
of the San Luis Valley..."*

CHAPTER THREE

FORT GARLAND ROSE from the high desert of the San Luis
Valley like a natural phenomenon. Constructed of adobe
bricks covered with hardened reddish-brown mud, it
melded into the landscape, looking more like a refuge for
owls and varmints than for blue-coated soldiers. From a
distance, only the vibrant colors of Old Glory flying above
the tiny parade ground identified it as being more than
just a jumble of windswept rocks set into the vast ero-
sional plain of the Rio Grande.

Viewed from the adjacent slopes of massive Mount
Blanca, the Fort seemed a small rectangular dike, a mere
windbreak set in the sage. From a practical perspective,
however, the Fort represented the power of the United
States of America and its attendant territories. It occupied
a strategic site at the eastern end of the San Luis Valley, at
the bottom of an immense saddle that bridged the
Continental Divide. On the eastern side were the
Huajatolla and the front range of the Rocky Mountains.
On the west was the gigantic expanse of the San Luis
Valley, ringed by the formidable Sangre de Cristo and San
Juan Mountains. Traversed by La Veta Pass, the great sad-
dle provided an acceptable route from the gold fields of
central Colorado, south along the Rio Grande to the

burgeoning trade route, the Santa Fe Trail.

Fort Garland existed to protect trade along the route, as well as to remind the Ute nation of its subservience to the White Father. The brain trust in Washington understood the significance of respect to the various Indian tribes, particularly those with complex, warlike societies like the Utes. For that reason, the U. S. government had to be represented in potentially hostile territory by someone of impeccable reputation among both whites and Indians. The first to come to General Philip Sheridan's mind was the legendary mountain man and scout, Kit Carson. Already a Colonel commanding a force that had broken the spirit of the Navajo, Carson was the hero of countless dime novels and a certifiable Western hero. Although he held no illusions concerning the mythical exploits attributed to Carson by the overexcited minds of lowbrow novelists, Sheridan knew that Carson's exploits were truly fabled among both Indians and whites.

Carson's orders caught up with him in New Mexico, and he soon crossed the Sangre de Cristos from Taos to Fort Garland, where he accepted the promotion to Brigadier General of the United States Army's Military Division of the Missouri with command over most of southern Colorado and northern New Mexico.

The general was an uncomfortable soldier, at best. Having joined the army as a scout at age 52, he longed for the days when he and Bridger scoured the Rockies for beaver, or when he and Joe Walker led John Frémont to hell and back. He felt uncomfortable in uniform, and often dressed in his soft buckskins or broadcloth civilian clothes.

The business with the Navajo had soured his enthusiasm for government work. The subjugation of the Navajo, culminating with the Indians' surrender in the bitter cold at Canyon de Chelly, weighed heavily on his mind. But with the war between the states finally over and adventurers turning their attentions to the West, the army had need of his frontier sensibilities. Besides, he reasoned that Fort Garland was close to family and friends at his Taos *hacienda.*

Perhaps the trailblazer's greatest pleasure was his proximity to his old friend, Sam Tate. Bridger was somewhere up in Wyoming these days, scouting for the railroad. Walker was still searching out new trails through the harsh Arizona deserts. Only Tate was nearby and could occasionally cross La Veta Pass to reminisce about the days of plentiful beaver and wild, unclaimed wilderness.

Carson was sitting in his quarters dictating a report on Ute activity to a young sergeant, when word arrived that Tate had been spotted riding up to the fort. He lightly brushed his graying moustache with his fingers, thinking that Tate had picked a curious time to cross the mountain saddle, only a few months after his previous visit. Usually Sam wasn't that sociable.

By the time Carson had dismissed the sergeant and called for one of the Mexican servants to prepare something to eat, he saw the squat figure of his old *compañero* pass by the dingy window, accompanied by Lieutenant Homer Keating. Keating had fought his way through skirmishes from Montana to Mexico, and was a good friend to one mountain man, an able subordinate to the other.

The rough-hewn door opened quickly and the two men stepped inside the sparsely furnished quarters.

"Howdy, Kit," said Tate, pulling his worn beaver hat from his head.

"Sam, you're a sight," answered Carson, grabbing Tate's hand and pumping it.

It was true. Tate stood eye to eye with Carson at a shade over five and a half feet. He was dressed in an ancient, sweatstained buckskin shirt, its intricate beadwork long worn away. The heavy cloth trousers were tucked into calf-high moccasins, worn to tough leather on the bottom.

Tate's grizzled face was both unique and captivating. Although of Irish and French ancestry, he had the proud, stoic look of the Indians he had both lived among and fought with. In fact, it was often said that he must have Indian blood. His high cheekbones and round face caused even the fierce Utes to feel a kinship. "Never was one to dazzle the eye, Kit."

Tate paused, pointed his thumb back over his shoulder toward the door, and shook his head.

"*Whaugh,* the fort's still growin'. Looks like the entire Union Army's bunked up along the river."

Carson snorted, then smiled.

"Gotta do somethin' with 'em after the war, Sam. They're out here to skeer the southern Ute nation into puttin' down their coup sticks and livin' peaceable."

He sighed heavily. "Mebbe me'n Ouray can do somethin' 'fore we all wind up kilt and sculpt."

The frontiersman looked to Lieutenant Keating.

"Homer, yee're welcome to stay and share a little tobaccee with me'n Sam, here."

"Thanks, general," answered Keating. He winked and said, "But when Kit Carson and Sam Tate start to powwow, I 'spect the lies'll be flyin' 'bout as thick as skeeters on the Yellerstone.

"I believe I'll go startle a few 'a them new young pups just arrived. See if'n there's any soldiers among 'em.

"Later, Sam...Kit."

The mountain men chuckled as Keating left the quarters, carefully closing the door behind him.

Tate looked long at his friend, and saw the toll the last few years had taken. The great frontiersman looked smaller, more frail than ever. Always diminutive, he was beginning to look shrunken. His eyes were deeply set and the wrinkles across his forehead spoke of some great strain. Tate grimly smiled to himself and thought that he must look the same.

The two companions sat in creaky wooden chairs at a polished pine table. Carson produced a small carved cedar box filled with aromatic tobacco and a hand-carved pipe. Tate reached inside his shirt, pulling out a buckskin pouch that housed his hardwood pipe. Both dipped their pipes into the tobacco and packed it hard into the bowls. Carson stood, walked to the hearth, and picked up a small fagot. Lighting it, he returned to the table where the friends lit their pipes and momentarily smoked in silence.

Their quiet mood was broken by a Mexican servant who brought homemade bitter ale and cornmeal *tamales*. The old friends pulled the corn husks from the *tamales* and sampled them, all the while bantering small talk back and forth.

Tate knew Carson wondered why he had come, but in the manner of both Indians and Mexicans, would never directly ask. Finally, he set aside his pipe and began.

"I ain't here to palaver, Kit."

"Didn't think so," answered Carson. "Ye look a mite riled."

"That I am," answered Tate. He steeled himself, then continued.

"Ye know them damn Garcias?"

Carson nodded, then snorted in disgust.

"Yup. Divils, all right. Shoulda kilt 'em a coupla years back. Woulda saved some grief up Canon City way."

Tate swallowed hard, sighed, and finally spoke the words.

"Woulda saved some grief out my way, too, Kit. They kilt Emily and young John," Tate paused. "Kilt Jed."

Forty years on the frontier, witnessing every kind of savagery, should have hardened Carson, made him immune to the suffering of a hard land. Sometimes it did. This time it did not.

"Aw, by damn," said Carson. "Ye can't have come with worse news, Sam."

Carson had known and respected Jed Gorner and fondly remembered Emily and her sister Mary as young, precocious girls. He knew how Tate treasured young John.

"John Francisco 'n Jake Herold brung me the news. Helped me bury 'em on that pretty little hill above the *Cucharas.*"

"Esther?" Carson queried.

"She'll handle it," he said grimly. "Got no other choice.

"Vasquez and his people are takin' her down to Chama to tell Mary 'n William."

Carson thought of his son and daughter-in-law, and how the news would cause Billy Carson to drop everything and set out after the outlaws.

"I know I ought to be with her, now," Tate continued. "But I cain't. I need to find them dogs that did the killin'."

His voice hardened, and the dark, bitter invective of his soul spilled out. "I got to see them divils skinned and set out to dry. Won't nothin' else do, Kit."

Carson shook his head in agreement.

"How do ye figure it happened, Sam?" he asked.

Tate related the story as told by Francisco and Herold, stopping frequently to let his rage subside.

"Finally, Esther and me rode on over to Jed 'n Emily's ranch 'n met that new preacher, Chastain. Jake 'n his boys had put together some fine coffins.

"Esther 'n me said our goodbyes. Preacher committed 'em to the ground. Not much more to say."

Tate stared at the cup on the table, surprised at how hard it was to talk to his old friend. In the back of his mind, he thought it curious that the two of them, who had survived every horror known to the frontier, could still be consumed by personal tragedy.

Carson looked older, frailer now than he had minutes ago. He knew the fury that rose in him had to be tempered by common sense, and he knew he must make sure Tate could see the situation clearly, also. He knew Tate had to talk about it.

"Ye say there's three of 'em, now?" asked Carson.

"Yup. Vivian and Filipio got a nephew ridin' with 'em name of Santiago. Guess he got too mean for the rest of the family down Albuquerque-way, so they sent him out with his uncles.

"Thinks he's a *bandido,*" Tate muttered. "Mebbe he is."

"Where ye figger they are now?" Carson asked.

"Three, mebbe four days ride north on the *Huerfano.* Jake scouted 'em out for eight, ten miles. Like I said, his youngest boy put a hole in Vivian, that godforsaken divil. Jake didn't think they hit Filipio or the nephew.

"They left sign that they were goin' to ground somewhere up north. I figure up by the gold strikes—Cripple Creek way."

Carson took in the information. "I thought they's workin' gold at Leadville, not down to the southern mountains."

"Whaugh. They're tearin' up every river you'n I ever took beaver off'n, Kit. Kate Patterson tells me there's more hard rock minin' going on now than there is in Boone's Kintucky."

Carson nodded in agreement, confirming his friendship with Decatur "Kate" Patterson. The flamboyant Georgian had come West with the Russell brothers, who wound up discovering gold in the foothills at the confluence of Cherry Creek and the South Platte River. The town they founded, Auraria, was now merged with its rival across the river, Denver.

Patterson and Green Russell had drifted up through the mountains, where Central City and Leadville were taking shape. Finally, they heeded the advice of Marion Merino and old Louis Vasquez and headed south to the *Huajatolla* country.

Honoring their southern sympathies when the War Between the States broke out, they attempted to lead a

33

group of Georgians back to fight for the confederacy via the Pecos River route. They were soon caught between Comanches on the warpath and the Union Army giving chase from Fort Union. Their choice was simple. They surrendered and sat out the war in New Mexico.

Patterson, in the meantime, made good use of this loose incarceration. He befriended many of the trappers and traders who made their living from the Santa Fe Trail, trading information about the gold fields for good will and occasionally a passable bottle of southern sour mash. When Patterson married one of the Georgia women, Martha Potts, while both were still in captivity, the Union soldiers anted up a $300 dowry and, at Ceran St. Vrain's request, resettled the couple near Francisco's Fort. Although a Georgian at heart, Patterson was also a pragmatist, and promised to sit out the rest of the war.

He turned out to be a reliable source of information for Carson following the war, as he kept in touch with the miners from Georgia who continued to search for the mother lode. It was Patterson who told Tate of the rich finds on Cripple Creek, and the probability of gold seekers flooding the southern Rockies.

Carson mulled over the information for a moment. "Kate's a pretty savvy feller. If there's miners 'n such crawling around those parts, them Garcias will be shootin' 'em up 'n pinchin' they pokes, no doubt."

He thought silently for a moment, then said, "We got to go after 'em, all right. Fort Dodge is too far and they's busy keepin' the peace on the Santa Fe Trail at Fort Union. That leaves us."

Tate looked at his friend and said, "It's God's honest truth, I was hopin' yee'd say that, Kit."

Carson favored his guest with a sad smile and said, "Oh, we'll git 'em, Sam."

"Yeah, we will. I'm a-gonna start myself right away, Kit, unless you got any better ideas."

34

"Well, Sam, somethin's weighin' on my mind, awright."

Carson picked up a leather courier's pouch from an adjacent desk and slapped it on the table.

"I just received orders to go down to Santa Fe—meet with the regimental brass over the Navajo business. Indian agent there's been treatin' 'em like orphan dogs, 'an I sent word to Washington. I got to attend an inquiry next week. Whole Division of the Missouri wants a report, and they want it now."

Tate's eyes widened at the news. He hadn't expected Carson to leave.

"Sam, I'm gonna send Homer along with a coupla Ute trackers after them weasels. When I get back, I'll join 'em as soon as I can."

"Kit," Tate began, only to have Carson wave his hand, silencing his friend.

"Now, lad, you and me, we've both tracked Messican bandits before, and you know as well as I they're slippery as bear grease. These Garcias 're more of the same, cept'n they're crazy for religion, I hear. Nothin' worse than scum that thinks God's on his side."

"I savvy," said Tate. "I heer'd Vivian was down on the Mogollon, sayin' he's been talkin' to Holy Mary, awright.

"I came here to talk this out. You know when yee're trackin' a divil cat, ye gotta think like one. It might look like they're headed north, but I 'spect they might make a cutback, mebbe over the front range and Pueblo and back by Garland here—try to head back south and get lost with some kin down to the Sandias.

"I'm plannin' on going back over the saddle to the Peaks, follow the *Cucharas* basin north. Mebbe Homer can go on over behind me. Him 'n his lads can follow the *Huerfano*."

Carson shook his head in agreement.

"My thinkin' exactly. Course, I always said ye could track a scorpion over a flat rock, Sam. 'Tween you 'n Homer, them divils is already vittles for the buzzards.

"Now, I heard the provisional gov'ner's put up a reward for the Garcias. Thousand dollars. Dead or alive, don't matter. Let's spread the word, mebbe get our work done for us."

Tate stood and stared out the window. The shadows were long toward the east.

"It's a hard time, Kit. I'm obliged for your help."

Carson absentmindedly ran his fingers over his moustache, twisting the ends, and made no direct reply. Finally, he said, "I'll call in Homer so's we can work up a plan."

Tate nodded in agreement. As Carson walked to the door to send a messenger for the lieutenant, Tate spoke.

"Kit, we've et many a beaver tail together. Broke a lotta trails. I want to ask ye to give Homer a direct order."

Carson turned around and raised an eyebrow.

"Name it," he said.

Tate looked at Carson, then mimicked pulling a knife and holding it out before him.

"If'n he gets to them butchers first," he said, and plunged the imaginary knife into his chest, "make sure he cuts out they black hearts."

*"...he saw a tiny whitewashed adobe church,
its only decoration a cross..."*

CHAPTER FOUR

THE PAIN IN HIS SHOULDER was gone, he realized. He rubbed
the area with the fingers of his right hand and could feel
nothing. Looking down, he opened the collar of the
clean white peasant's blouse and saw that the grievous
wound had completely healed.

He looked quizzically down at his bare feet, planted
firmly in the warm sand, and thought he was far from his
home. He knew he should be returning.

He began walking, his white blouse and pants billowing
in the mild southwest breeze. He could feel his long hair
being fanned by the wind, and indulged in its coolness. He
wore no hat, and was puzzled as to its whereabouts.
Perhaps it was with his brother, who seemed to have disappeared, also.

Out of habit, he reached with his right hand across his
body in search of his pistol. He found nothing.

He continued to walk across the interminable high
desert, feeling certain that he was growing nearer and
nearer to his village. Although the rough ground was
strewn with sharp stones and yucca spines, he knew
they would do him no harm, for his journey had great
significance.

The panorama before him was vast and slightly

foreboding. In the distance, off to the southeast, the Sandia Range rose out of the desert floor. The mountain's lush foliage reflected bright green against the azure sky, and he had to squint his eyes to take in its radiance.

He kept walking.

At some point, a coyote sneaked from the protective cover of a grove of pinon pines and began circling him, staggering from fatigue every few steps. The wild dog was panting from thirst, its tongue rapidly flicking in and out of its mouth as it gasped for air. Its ribs were nearly poking through its mottled hide. He was amazed the dog could even stand.

"Hola, Coyote," he said, bending over and reaching out his hand. He hoped the animal would come, so he could smooth its fur, and perhaps feel the blood pounding through its mangy body. He wanted to soothe the beast.

The coyote remained at a distance and warily sat on its skinny haunches, watching the man. Finally, Vivian stood upright and started walking once again, and the unsteady wild dog settled in behind.

In the distance he saw a tiny whitewashed adobe church, its only decoration a cross carved from a willow, its crossbeams bound by sisal rope. The cross was set into the apex of the church's roof and seemed to reflect the fire of the impending sunset in the west.

As he neared, he saw the rough plank door of the church was open, and many candles were burning on the tiny, immaculate altar. He stopped in the doorway for a moment, and looked around to see the coyote sitting back along the trail, panting and drooling into the sand.

When he turned forward, he realized he stood at the threshold of the tiny church, and was astonished at the smooth texture of the adobe and the radiance of the white paint. This was truly a place of God.

He entered the dim sanctuary and slowly walked to the altar, seeing that the candles ringed a silver bowl. The vessel held liquid he assumed to be holy water, blessed by the Savior. He stood before the bowl for a moment to get his bearings, then knelt on the hard-packed dirt floor, bowed his head and began to pray out loud. His open eyes noticed his long hair hanging toward his cupped hands, then they inadvertently followed a deep crack in the floor that snaked between his knees. He felt that it was somehow imperceptibly growing, widening into a chasm. He was alarmed.

Suddenly, as he had somehow expected, the sanctuary slowly began to brighten. He continued to stare at his folded hands and saw the grimy, scarred fingers slowly emerge from shadow into incandescence. He prayed harder, imploring the Lord for both courage and wisdom. In a few moments, the light was nearly too much to bear, yet his heart was filled to overflowing with anticipation.

He knew this had happened before. He knew what to expect.

Finally, he heard the voice. Speaking in perfect, formal Castilian, it seemed a cool spring that appears from beneath desert sands, a loving touch from a long lost mother, a piece of heaven.

"Look upon me, Vivian. Look upon the holy mother of God."

He slowly lifted his head and allowed the light to bathe his face. He could feel the tears running down his cheeks and into his beard as the form of the Blessed Virgin took shape before him.

She stood beside the small altar, her hands held before her with palms upward in supplication. She was resplendent in luminous white and blue satin robes, from under which perfect, tiny feet appeared. Hers was such exquisite beauty that he was unable to move his eyes

41

from her face, even to blink.

He was enchanted.

The Virgin Mary favored Vivian Garcia with a beatific smile, holding him in complete subjugation. She slowly inverted her hands, reached out and lightly touched the crown of his head.

He felt her power stream through him and remembered that sometime, not long ago, he had been chosen.

"Dear Vivian," she said. "Am I not the Savior's mother?"

"Yes, holy Virgin," he answered with authority, knowing it to be true.

"I come again to you with the word of God. You are blessed unto Him. You are blessed unto the holy saints. You are blessed unto me."

The tears gushed from his eyes as he felt her benevolence.

"Your mission will continue and grow, dear Vivian. Those who have harmed you will be punished by my hand. Those who come to take this blessed land must also be punished.

"You are my instrument, Vivian."

The phrase seemed to take on a life of its own, floating into the air, becoming all encompassing. Its echo filled his every sense with transcendent vibration. He was her instrument. *The* Instrument.

He found that he was looking back down at the ground, at the widening crack between his knees. He was alarmed at how rapidly it grew, and the low rumbling sound it made. He felt it would surely swallow him. He quickly snapped his head back up to implore the Virgin to stem the widening fissure. He gasped with shock when he saw that she had disappeared, as had the holy light that surrounded her. He saw only the smoke rising from each of the extinguished candles on the altar.

Panicking, his eyes returned downward, where he saw

42

that his wound had opened. The blood gushed from his maimed shoulder and splattered the ground, seeping into the expanding crack and filling it to the brim. He reached to cover the wound with his hand, and realized that he held a cocked and loaded pistol.

Suddenly, all was black, and he struggled to find the holy light of the Virgin. He willed himself upward, upward, through the ceiling, to the sky, where her light might be found.

Upward, upward.

The pain was exquisite. His shoulder felt as if a stake had been driven through it, pinning him to the grimy blanket that covered the saddle against which he lay. Similarly, his leg felt as if skinning knife had laid it open.

He groggily lifted his head and blinked his eyes repeatedly, simultaneously shaking off the dream and clearing his tears of pure rapture. The pain left him mere moments to relish the precious memory of the Virgin that had come to him in his delirium, induced by fever and cheap whiskey.

Vivian Garcia lay propped up against a pinon pine. Hidden at the bottom of a shallow, brushy ravine, he could see the sky beginning to show the first hint of dawn, the rosy pink light bathing the rimrock above. The overwhelming pain caused his mind to clear instantly, and he remembered the long ride, north up the Huerfano Valley to the hidden gully. He had recovered from the initial numbing shock of being shot, and the pain had set in. His shoulder carried the slug from the ambush at Herold's, and he had prayed during his fleeting moments of consciousness for death to come, for the pain to stop. Yet, each prayer went unanswered, and his horse's rocking gait continued to shoot fire through his body.

Finally, the outlaws stopped to make camp. Vivian was lifted from his injured horse, screaming as Filipio and Santiago laid him on a thatch of pine branches, then screaming once again as they placed him against the stiff, stolen saddle they removed from the horse.

The first night was pure hell, a mixture of excruciating pain followed by blackouts filled with frenzied nightmares. Fearing those who might follow, the outlaws made no fire, so Vivian was denied even the small comfort of warm water to bathe his wound. His nephew had merely covered the hole with a dirty rag to stop the bleeding.

The delirium had set in the next morning. His brother tried to keep him quiet by pouring whiskey down his throat, but to no avail. Finally, in an effort to stop both his screaming and his chattering teeth, a stout stick was forced sideways between his jaws and tied in place with piece of rope around his head.

The next two days were an agonizing blur. In between torturous bouts of alternating chills and raging fever, he recalled the stick being removed long enough for whiskey to be poured down his throat. He also remembered Filipio changing the dressing on the wound, pulling the scabbed cloth away, only to start the bleeding anew. A new cloth was laid over the wound, and the stick was removed from his mouth. Now, it was the fourth day following the shooting, and as he returned to consciousness, his hatred for Jake Herold was as absolute as the pain in his body. The *gringo* had dared to refuse the Garcias their needed supplies. A hidden assassin had shot him. They had persecuted the Virgin's chosen Instrument. He would kill them all. He gazed at the lightening sky and knew that his hate had been blessed by the Virgin, for she had told him his cause was just.

"Once again, Blessed Virgin," he silently prayed, "you have visited your servant.

"I will kill the *gringos,* for they have sinned against your people. I will kill. I will *kill."*

He grimaced as he slowly shifted his weight to the right, allowing him to survey the camp area. A groan escaped his parched lips and he squeezed his eyes tightly shut. Time froze as he willed the pain to subside. Finally, he opened his eyes and looked over the camp.

In the shadow light, he saw two blanket-wrapped forms lying in a clump of pines some fifteen yards away. Behind them, across a foot-wide brook, the outlaws' horses were picketed in a small, grassy clearing.

"Filipio," he croaked.

Immediately, the two blankets exploded into the air. The older bandido bolted into a crouch, his pistol pointed directly at Vivian. The younger slithered like a scorpion for several feet toward the horses, then also came up with a pistol.

Vivian stared at his two companions, locking eyes with each. He communicated softly, without words. They saw the holy zeal in his eyes and knew that he was back from the dead.

"Water," he whispered, his voice cracking.

The younger outlaw quickly headed for his bedroll and produced a canteen. He filled it at the brook, then returned to Vivian and slowly tipped the vessel toward his uncle's mouth. Most of the water rolled off his bearded chin onto his neck and chest. Finally, he held a mouthful and slowly swallowed. He felt the liquid sliding down his parched throat, its pain minor compared to that in his shoulder. He felt it bring life.

Filipio Garcia stood across the clearing and watched the boy administer the water to his brother. His eyes were narrowed as he calculated that his brother would likely rejoin the living after all.

He was profoundly disappointed.

After Vivian had managed to swallow five or six gulps

of water, he leaned back to his original position, grimacing and clenching his teeth. Fighting to regain control, he breathed heavily through his nose. Finally, he looked at the other gunmen, and spoke.

"I have talked with the Virgin," he said with conviction.

Filipio and Santiago exchanged nervous looks. Vivian was well known for talking with the Virgin, and each time he became more distant, more adamant in his fervor to follow what he said was God's will.

"She has once again blessed me," he continued. His weary eyes began to flutter as he fought to remain conscious. Losing the battle, he drifted off, speaking slowly and slurring his words.

"We will keep avenging our people. We will kill Herold. I...the Virgin told me to...I am her Instrument."

Vivian's head lolled to the side, and his body slowly returned to its previous position against the saddle. Filipio and Santiago quickly began breaking camp, rolling their blankets into bedrolls and strapping them onto their saddles. Filipio grunted as he shouldered his heavy saddle and carried it to his picketed horse. He calmed the skittish animal with a soothing song and was soon tightening the ancient leather cinch around the horse's belly.

The boy watched Filipio warily. When the older outlaw finished saddling his horse, he walked back to the camp and motioned to the boy.

"Saddle your horse," he said.

The boy hid his surprise well. He hesitated, his hooded eyes challenging his uncle.

Filipio's piercing stare quelled any rebelliousness in his nephew, and the boy dropped his eyes.

"A precaution. We must be ready, Santiago. Jake Herold and others are surely following. We can wait no longer."

"We can stand against the *gringo*," the boy said

spitefully.

Filipio laughed bitterly.

"Perhaps. But he will be aided by a Spirit."

"A Spirit?"

"Yes. I've been thinking these past days. Thinking of a name Herold spoke. Gorner."

The outlaw saw the confusion in the boy's face. Santiago merely shook his head, indicating that he did not understand.

"Vivian was unwise in his choice of...," Filipio hesitated momentarily, "targets. The name Gorner holds significance, nephew. Great meaning.

"The woman who fought like a wildcat was the *Spirit's* daughter. The daughter of Sam Tate."

Santiago's eyes grew wide in shock and surprise, and he sputtered, "Sam Tate? *Aiee.*"

Filipio waited for the news to sink in, for the fear to grip the boy. Finally, he spoke.

"Some believe Tate can track the wind over the water. Maybe it is so."

He spoke bitterly. "I have waited these four days, thinking of a plan. We can wait no longer. If we want to live to carry out Vivian's *mission,*" he spat the word, "we must keep moving. Tate will know we seek to disappear on the Sandia, so we must not go there yet.

"I hear of gold in the Sangre de Cristos. We'll ride north and cross from the Pueblo on the Arkansas into the gold fields. We'll take gold from miners and return to the Sandia when word reaches Tate. By the time he gets there, we'll have returned down the Huerfano, crossed La Veta Pass by the *Huajatolla,* and be headed south to the Sandia."

"But Fort Garland is there," said Santiago. "The soldiers will be tracking us. Carson and Tate are like brothers, are they not?"

"Yes, they will track us. But once we kill a few miners

[handwritten margin note, left:] Class Part 12/2

[handwritten margin note, right:] Vivian's bandidos may not actually be very logal

47

to the north, they will go there, while we slip by them on our way home."

Santiago slowly absorbed the information while Filipio reached into a deerskin pouch, pulled out a piece of dried beef, and began chewing the tough meat. The boy gently pulled on the soft, fine hair of his upper lip, thinking frantically.

"But what about Vivian?" he asked. "He cannot ride."

"Vivian *must* ride," answered Filipio. "We will strap him on his horse and stop to rest when we can.

"Perhaps his Virgin will give him comfort."

Filipio ordered the boy to build a small, hidden fire beneath a heavily-leafed willow and make some broth for Vivian. He then mounted his horse and rode a soft, grassy trail up out of the arroyo to scout the area.

He stopped at the rim and slowly surveyed the quickly-lightening horizon. Seeing no sign of danger, he rode out of the draw, moving in concentric circles around the campsite, searching for any indication of pursuit.

He ran across the remains of a week-old Cheyenne camp along a spring a mile to the east, and saw that the group had headed northeast, toward the Arkansas River. He found no other sign.

Riding back to the hidden camp, he zigzagged across the rough country, half prairie and half foothills. The mixture of scrub oak, pinon pine, and sagebrush reminded him of his home, the country at the base of the Sandias.

He will be there soon enough, he thought. Then Vivian could pray while he and Santiago pursued new adventures.

Vivian's holy crusade against Anglo settlers was the result of a double-cross turned murder by white traders. Twenty-three year-old Vivian and his friend, Pedro Herrera, had been hired by the traders to drive supply wagons from the southern part of the New Mexico Territory up to the Santa Fe Trail. When they arrived at the outskirts of Santa Fe, they were ambushed by one of the traders intent on selling the stock himself. Herrera was killed instantly by a ball from a single shot rifle. The trader then pulled a pistol and aimed it directly at Vivian's chest. When it misfired, Vivian jumped from the wagon and sprinted through the cholla and sage. Hearing the trader's pursuit, he fled into a dry riverbed and ran for several miles before reaching a patch of stony ground where he could lose the pursuit. He wound up hiding under a low cutbank until nightfall, when he emerged and walked south to his village in the shadow of the Sandias.

It was on that moonlit trek that Vivian had his first vision of the Blessed Virgin Mary. As he later related, he was weak with thirst and had fallen to the ground in despair. A great light suddenly appeared, and the Virgin stood before him. In a beautiful, musical voice, she told him he was to avenge the murder of Pedro Herrera. The *gringos* had offended her and spilled blood on holy ground. She then disappeared as quickly as she had come.

Vivian walked the remaining miles to the village, his heart soaring. He was found lying face up on the outskirts of the village, totally exhausted and badly dehydrated. He was praying and, some said, speaking to someone who was not there.

When he recovered, he told Filipio of his amazing encounter, and of the Virgin's instruction to seek vengeance. Filipio eagerly joined his brother's quest. At 19, he had been fond of both drink and women and had bullied virtually everyone in the village except his older brother. He saw Vivian's wondrous vision as an opportunity for adventure.

It often occurred to Filipio that his brother was *loco*.

Their mother had said as much when Vivian told her of the Virgin's visit, when he told her he was God's sword.

"The Virgin tells you to kill nothing, Vivian," she had said. "The Blessed Mary's Son is a God of life, not of death. You see nothing but Satan in the guise of our Savior's mother.

"Do not listen to him, Vivian. Do not do the devil's work."

Filipio had listened with interest, chuckling inside. He knew the Virgin had not come to Vivian. Nor had the Dark Prince. He knew that Vivian had always been disturbed, eager to follow causes and to seek God's favor. Now, he had an excuse.

Filipio needed no justification. From the time of his childhood, it was said that while he was quick in mind, he lacked compassion, that he could not realize the joy in life. In his rare moments of thinking about this coldness of soul, he supposed that he agreed. Yet he could not perceive that something was missing, for he had never felt it, never experienced different emotions. Viciousness and compassion were abstract concepts. They were merely used as means to various ends.

He did not believe in Vivian's Virgin. But he did believe—as much as he could—in the mission. Killing settlers, stealing their money and possessions, raping the women—all appealed to Filipio, all made him *feel* something.

Filipio had joined his brother's campaign against Anglo settlers, and the pair rode north into Colorado, where they ambushed a near-destitute rancher on the Arkansas, setting fire to his shack and killing his livestock. They tied the wounded man to a fence post and left him to die.

They were new at the game. They made mistakes. The rancher managed to hold onto life and was found a day later by a band of Arapahoe who had seen the smoke from the fire. They transported the wounded man to a settlement on the Huerfano, where he described his attackers before dying three days later.

The provisional government of the Territory of Colorado issued a description of the attackers, implying that a reward might be forthcoming for their capture. The equivocal nature of the communication caused many old timers to shake their heads and laugh. The wry old mountain man Jim Baker summed it up when he said, "This child ain't leavin' home nor hearth. The gum'mint ain't gonna pay bull barley fer a coupla dead Messicans."

The government's charge went unanswered while the Garcias perfected their trade. Over the next three years, 21 more settlers, miners, and soldiers were ambushed and killed by the Garcias. During that time, they became less selective in their choice of victims. Many were Mexican, half were Filipio's chosen prey—women. Filipio was heard to brag in many New Mexico *cantinas* that the brothers didn't even bother to count their Indian victims.

The brothers' murders ranged throughout southern Colorado and northern New Mexico. They killed three miners near the new settlement of Canon City, near the rugged and spectacular gorge of the Arkansas.

They ambushed a supply wagon at Chama, killing both the guard and driver. They never recognized the driver as Ramon Sanchez, their own cousin.

Vivian killed out of religious fanaticism. Filipio killed merely out of adventure. They had yet to kill the wrong person.

On one trip back to their village in the shadow of the Sandias, Filipio was approached by the bastard son of their unmarried sister. Their nephew Santiago, barely sixteen, had nearly killed another boy in a dispute over a girl. He was an outcast. Filipio saw some of himself in the boy's eyes, and when the Garcias rode out again into the dusty desert, the boy came along.

The provisional governor finally succumbed to public pressure, and offered a reward of $1,000 for the capture of the Garcia Gang, dead or alive. About the same time, Vivian's holy passion took the gang over La Veta Pass and down the *Cucharas* River. They chose a neat, expansive ranch with a pasture surrounded by wire, an oddity the desperados had not seen before. Waiting until dawn, they slowly rode up to the small barn, where a man and boy were busy preparing to shoe a horse. Vivian shot the man immediately. The unshod horse shot past the outlaws in a panicked gallop.

The man still managed to turn and come up with a rifle, shooting at Vivian and spooking his mount. The horse backed away wildly into the rough wire which lacerated its flank and tore into Vivian's leg.

Filipio continued shooting, wounding the man further. Finally, their victim dropped the rifle and toppled to the ground. The young boy had taken off toward a grove of cottonwoods growing on the banks of a small brook. Excitedly, Santiago quickly aimed his rifle at the boy's back and shot. The boy rolled twice before coming to a stop.

Santiago looked to his uncles for praise, only to see Vivian trying to control his panicked horse and Filipio bearing down on a woman who had appeared from the adjacent house.

Filipio jumped from his horse and slammed the woman to the ground. He dragged her up and slapped her before hauling her into a tack shed near the barn.

Vivian and Santiago ransacked the house before finally dousing the floors and walls with lamp oil. Outside, Vivian allowed Santiago to light a lamp and throw it into the house, and the structure went up like kindling.

Filipio appeared from the tack shed, disheveled and

panting. He grabbed his horse's reins and jumped into the saddle. He smiled briefly at the others, and waited for them to mount and ride.

Vivian was beside himself, cursing the strange wire. His leg was bleeding badly, as was the horse's flank. He pulled a bottle of whiskey from his saddle pack, poured it onto the gaping wound and cursed even more vehemently, all the while calling on his precious Virgin to ease the pain.

Vivian entered the tack shed and reemerged with a new, highly polished saddle. He favored his brother with an evil look and spat on the ground before removing his old saddle, throwing it to the ground, and slipping the new saddle on his wounded horse's back.

Filipio watched his brother with growing disgust. The constant religious babbling had run its course with the younger brother, and he knew that some sort of conflict between them was inevitable.

Finally, after picking up the dead man's rifle and slipping it in a scabbard attached to the saddle, Vivian led the group out of the spread's surrounding yard and onto the prairie. He knew Herold's Crossing was near. There would be medicine and food. The ride was likely less than an hour, and although a trading post could be foolhardy to attack, perhaps it was time for chances to be taken.

After all, what were a few more dead *gringos?*

Now, on his horse returning to the arroyo camp, Filipio reflected on the absolute reality that surrounded the killing of the Gorner woman. He still bore the marks of her fingers on his neck. She had fought like a demon to resist her violation and murder, but in the end was not strong enough. He felt no remorse, and in fact was excited by the memory of her struggle. Yet, he knew that they had finally overstepped their bounds. When Jake Herold had uttered the Gorner name in the yard of his

53

trading post, Filipio was startled. He had heard the name before, and slowly remembered that it held significance. Finally, he pieced together a jumble of impressions and memories and came to the jarring conclusion that the woman he murdered was the daughter of Sam Tate. By killing her, he had surely unleashed the Spirit of Death.

Tate's name was spoken in whispers, with reverence and awe. It was said that perhaps only Bridger could equal Tate in tracking the slightest sign. Even the Apache, with their almost supernatural ability to blend in with the land, expressed admiration for the old tracker, and talked of him as a mighty warrior.

Filipio felt something odd, an emotion he had never experienced. It nagged him—made him uneasy and angry. When he thought of Sam Tate, his heart beat faster. He found himself swallowing uncontrollably. His breathing was shallow. It was indeed a strange sensation. He had no way of knowing that others called it fear.

The arroyo camp was quiet when he returned, the small fire already doused by Santiago. The boy had some-how managed to move Vivian into an upright position against the pine, and removed the saddle. The outlaw's head gently swayed from side to side as he struggled to stay conscious. Both horses stood saddled and ready to ride.

Filipio dismounted and knelt next to his brother. He moved close, ignoring the stench of the wounded man's breath, and spoke into his ear.

"Vivian," he said. "We must ride. We must ride now."

Vivian's eyes slowly opened and focused. He chuckled wryly.

"Ride? How can I ride? I cannot even sit.

"No, Filipio, we cannot ride."

He paused, turned his head and looked directly at his brother. He spoke in ragged rhythm, his voice cracked from both thirst and lack of use.

"I have seen the Virgin, talked with her once again. I was walking to our village, lost in the desert. A shrine was before me. As I prayed, she appeared and told me...told me to continue."

He looked directly at his brother, his eyes filled with holy fervor.

"I am her Instrument, Filipio," he said weakly.

Filipio cupped Vivian's face with both hands, forcing his brother to pay attention.

"*Listen,* brother," he said vehemently. "Your Virgin has not done well by us. You lay here in fever, shot by someone we could not even see.

"No, your Virgin is not with us now. She would have warned us about the ranch on the *Cucharas,* eh? She would have warned us about the woman whose man and boy we left lying in the sun, wouldn't she?"

Vivian attempted to shake his head, to show that he didn't understand. Filipio's iron grip held him firm.

"No, you don't understand, do you, Vivian? That woman, she was surely death's daughter."

The older outlaw merely gave Filipio a questioning stare.

"The name, Vivian, the name Jake Herold spoke. *Gorner.* Does it mean anything to you?"

Slowly, almost imperceptibly, an awareness came over Vivian's features. His eyes suddenly filled with shock.

"Tate?" he whispered weakly. "Sam Tate's people?"

"Yes, Vivian," said Filipio.

"And now you understand. So we ride. We ride to the gold fields, where there is no way for Tate to track our sign. We will outrun the devil."

"I cannot," said Vivian defiantly.

"Then you will stay here alone, and meet Tate's vengeance face to face."

Filipio released his brother's face and stood.

"Santiago, we go now, " he said to the boy.

He paced purposefully toward his horse and raised his foot into the stirrup. The boy hung back, then also began to mount.

"Wait," said Vivian. He struggled to sit upright against the pine. His face had become a vision of determination, his holy passion focused on the mission. Yet, something had changed. He had killed with impunity, yet rarely out of personal vengeance. Now, he required that fierce retribution. The very core of him demanded it.

Slowly, with incredible effort, he pulled his legs up underneath him, and struggled to his knees. Extending his left hand to Filipio, he met his brother's eyes with a ferocious look.

"The Virgin has told me to continue," he said. "Help me stand."

Filipio grabbed the outstretched hand and pulled Vivian up, wrapping his arm under the wounded out-law's good arm and around his back. The effort caused sweat to break out on Vivian's forehead, but his gaze remained steady.

He worked his tongue around his mouth, trying to wet his lips.

"Bring me water, then tie me to the saddle so I will not fall.

"We ride, Filipio," he said vehemently, his eyes filled with hate. "But we ride for Jake Herold."

*"Thunderheads towered like sentinels
over the front range..."*

CHAPTER FIVE

THUNDERHEADS TOWERED like sentinels over the front range, ready to release their burden down countless mountain gullies. They roiled and churned in the early afternoon sky, quickly covering up the clear blue, pushing it to the east.

Sam Tate sat motionless astride his stallion, his face turned skyward to the black clouds. He sniffed the moisture laden breeze and wiped the back of his hand across his mouth.

"Aye, Tom," he said aloud to the horse, "We're in for a drownin', we are.

"Damned divils've found a piece of luck, old hoss," he said bitterly.

"May as well hole up and wait fer the wash. Can't track sign in the mud."

Tate led the horse to a rock outcropping situated on the side of a small arroyo. Huge drops of rain began splattering the ground as they took shelter. By the time the mountain man had dismounted and leaned back against the rock shelf, a full-fledged storm surrounded them

Tate looked out at the torrent and cursed his luck. A storm of this magnitude would erase most of the Garcias' back trail he had hoped to follow.

He left Fort Garland the morning after his meeting with Carson and headed directly across La Veta Pass for the

Cucharas River, stopping at Francisco's Fort only long enough to leave word of his doings for Esther. He then made his way down to Herold's Crossing where he met with Jake Herold, outlining his plans for tracking the killers. He told Herold to keep an eye out for Homer Keating's party, which would likely follow the Cucharas to the Crossing before heading northwest to the Huerfano.

It had not taken him long to pick up the trail leading from Herold's Crossing. Even days later the group's panicked flight was etched on the land. Three horses in full flight across the fragile prairie tended to stir up the countryside, and Tate followed the trail as if it were a boulevard in St. Louis.

The story of the outlaws' hard ride was written in the soil, punctuated by deep hoof imprints and scattered dirt. Tate knew that following such a trail required little expertise, and surmised that the trio's tracks would soon become harder to follow, reflecting a more careful nature after the outlaws felt they had outdistanced any initial pursuit. They had ridden hard for the first few miles, Tate discovered. Then they had slowed down, alternately trotting and walking. Although the ants and flies had evidently removed most of the blood lost by either man or horse, Tate still ran across enough splashed on rocks to know that Vivian Garcia was seriously wounded. Young Amos Herold's aim was true.

But now the storm had come, and a Colorado gullywasher it was. These quick but violent storms were common, boiling up in midafternoon, only to pass through in an hour or so, leaving the countryside fresh and the sky once again a sparkling blue.

Tate stood under the outcropping, put his rough hands over his face, and rubbed his eyes. Dressed in old buckskins that took on the color of the surrounding country, he fiddled with the newly-acquired Navy Colt tucked into a makeshift holster attached to his belt. To him, the pistol was only insurance, a weapon to be used in emergencies and nothing else. Like most men of the West, he remained true to his first love, the rifle. Tate carried both a Sharps .50 caliber, commonly known as a buffalo gun, and a newer Henry .44 repeating rifle. The Sharps had slowly eclipsed the old standby Hawken carried by most mountain men 30 years earlier. Although heavy and unwieldy, when used properly it was a deadly instrument of destruction. The Henry was no less so, a stout weapon with lever action, capable of picking off its target with lethal accuracy at over 250 yards.

Tate bought the Sharps in St. Louis, following his first foray into the Shining Mountains. He had left the Mississippi a mere boy and returned a hardened frontiersman. The rifle had been with him ever since, an extension of himself. Together, they had traveled from Canada to Mexico, and had beheld the endless blue waters of the Pacific. In Carson's service, the rifle had cut a deadly swath in the Kiowa and Comanche at the second Adobe Walls conflict. It had provided meat to vast numbers of Sheridan's troops. Like the Hawken it replaced, it had saved Tate's life at least a dozen times. And now he meant for it to exact a terrible revenge.

Carson had indicated that the Colorado territorial government issued a reward for the capture of the Garcias, dead or alive. Tate had no intention of exercising the latter option. His plan was to find them and kill them as mercilessly as possible. Although he could not know it, his mission was every bit as urgent and ruthless as Vivian Garcia's.

Waiting for the rain to play itself out, Tate allowed himself to think deeply for the first time about the events of the past few days. He had reacted spontaneously up until now, out of instinct it seemed. He had not truly taken time to grieve, and now he felt his self-control slipping away.

The whole of his life stood out before him at that

moment like some weird mental panorama. The defining events of his existence were equally accessible, not subject to any standard chronology. He saw how they were intertwined, how each affected the other. He saw his life as a series of reactions to a single decision. He had heeded the call and gone West. Everything else hinged on that one action, and his world had formed around it.

This bittersweet musing was new to him. A practical man, he rarely allowed himself the luxury of reflection. In the early years, to do so would likely have been fatal. Daydreaming invited a brightly colored Blackfeet arrow, or a frenzied she-griz.

As he aged, his life remained full of adventure which, combined with ingrained habit, effectively prohibited a view of his life's fabric. He had no time to put his existence into perspective. He was too busy constructing a legend.

Now, under this furious downpour, he saw it all with absolute clarity, and his life's grief seemed overwhelming. The pain that he felt at the death of his daughter and her family was matched by only one other occasion, and for the first time in decades, he allowed himself to remember his life with the Snake, his life with Bright Star.

Already an accomplished man of the mountains at the age of 23, he knew the Indians were keeping watch on his activities as he trapped beaver throughout the streams west of the Yellowstone country. When three young Snake warriors finally made contact, he was shocked at the easy rapport they developed. Using common sign language, trading was done, tobacco was shared, and the new round-eyes was allowed to trap without interference. Following a devastating early fall blizzard, Tate was given shelter with the tribe and lived with them for nearly two seasons.

Early on, while learning the Shoshoni tongue, he noticed a young woman of the tribe, a girl really, whose averted eyes often assessed the young round-eyes when she thought he wasn't looking. As is the way of such things, Tate and Bright Star soon lived in the same lodge. She was the perfect Snake wife—attentive, proud, and fiercely protective of her husband. He was head over heels in love.

Tate learned the ways of the Snake, and even participated in raids on rival tribes. He evidenced an innate ability for tracking, and soon was bestowed the name Many Hunts for his ability at providing game.

When he packed up his beaver pelts and headed for the great Green River Rendezvous, his future extended only as far as the Snake camp. Upon his return, everything had changed. Two fevered Frenchmen had approached the camp. Although they were turned away and died in the wild, the disease they had brought with them spread throughout the camp.

Bright Star lived only three days after Tate's return, and died in agony. In her semi-consciousness, she professed her devotion to her great husband, Many Hunts. He could only stare, helpless and silent. He joined in the death chants of the Shoshoni.

Tate immediately entered the wilderness, heading north and trapping for the next year. He shunned everything human and honed his tracking skills until they comprised a sixth sense. He intuitively knew when either trappers or Indians were near, and avoided them like the plague that killed Bright Star. For their part, the Crow and Gros Ventre occasionally caught sign of this white ghost, but could not catch sight.

Finally, his grief gradually coming undone, he knew he must re-enter the world. When he reappeared, he learned from Bridger that the fur trade was playing out, that his plews were virtually worthless. He sold them for what little he could, saddled up and headed east down the Missouri River, back to St. Louis.

He didn't intend to see the Shining Mountains again. Yet,

he found himself telling stories of the Popo Agie rendezvous to his father and sisters. While working over the forge at Sauters Smithy, he sometimes felt an absolutely physical need to inhale the pristine air of the Sangre de Cristos. And often, while talking in low secretive tones to an attentive young woman named Esther Maggs, he couldn't contain his excitement when describing the majestic peaks of the Rocky Mountains.

It was only a matter of time before he returned to the Western frontier, his adventurous new wife at his side. They settled in with the Spanish community of the *Cucharas*. Colorado would be their home.

It was only now, these many years later, that Tate allowed himself to once again feel the grief that drove him to a solitary year in the northern mountains. He knew this nostalgic pain was fueled by the Garcia's savagery, that his memory opened up in response to this new anguish. But his life since the Snake had hardened him, imbuing him with a stoicism that was necessary on the rough frontier.

Tate realized that while the agony of Bright Star's death had been astonishing, it had not been fueled by hate or rage. And therein lay the fundamental motivation for his quest. This new grief was complicated. It required action. It resulted in raw emotions that flowed into one another like drops of water—love, hate, regret, grief and vengeance. Surely vengeance.

The sight of his daughter resting in the pine coffin was almost unbearable. She had so much of Esther's patience and common sense, yet she cultivated and cherished a carefree, almost wild streak from both Tate and her "Uncle" Kit. She had surely died fighting, and for that Tate was grateful.

If humanly possible, young John Gorner's body evoked even more passion in the tracker. Although not a demonstrative man, Tate had adored his grandson. The boy displayed his mother's wit and style, yet was his father's son, wed to the land. Tate held the young boy's lifeless hand as he stared at the body of Jed Gorner and vowed to settle matters properly.

Sam Tate's hate was near palpable. He could taste it. But being a man of the mountains, he refused to let it drive him, refused to let it make him rash. He reckoned all the hate in the world was useless if it did not result in vengeance. So he retained the careful nature that had saved his life so many times. He fought back the urge to hurry, to disregard caution. He would follow the Garcias' trail until it ended. Then they would die. If he did not find them before Homer or Kit, then they would die just as surely from the guns of his friends.

Tate gingerly reached into the *possibles* sack strapped around his midsection and stared straight ahead as his fingers searched for a familiar shape. He pulled out a locket, one of three that generally rested on a chest alongside the bed he and Esther had shared these many years. Each carried a photograph. One was of Esther, the other two of their daughters. Looking down now, he pulled the locket open and looked upon the image of his younger daughter, Emily. He was struck anew by her beauty, by the presence she carried about her. Even the stern look with which she had favored the photographer could not hide the spirit she possessed. The dark upswept hair accented her determined face, and her full lips and remarkable eyes caused currents of pain to run through his heart. For the first time since her death, he wept. He wept with an overwhelming agony he thought he could no longer possess. He wept hard and long, and found he could not control himself. He wept from passion. He wept from loss. He wept from fury. The vermin who had killed her would pay dearly, he vowed. They would pay for Tate's tears.

A sudden, all-encompassing hush fairly tore him from his musing. The roar of the storm had ceased so abruptly that the absence of sound was nearly painful. His ears adjusted to the silence, picking up only the sound of water dripping from the rock overhang into puddles below.

He waited a few minutes, then closed the locket and returned it to his bag before walking the stallion out from under the overhang. A line of dazzling blue sky was peeking over the mountains to the west, and Tate reckoned on four more hours of daylight. He mounted the horse and spurred it up out of the shallow arroyo, into the muddy foothills leading to the broad Colorado prairie.

The rain had obliterated the obvious trail taken by the outlaws, yet Tate guessed correctly that their frenzied flight would leave less noticeable signs not so easily wiped out. Scouting back and forth across a broad plain, he found a patch of buffalo grass ripped from the ground, obviously by horses' hooves. A few hundred yards to the northeast, a pine branch was dangling from the tree. Still further, several lichen-covered stones were disrupted.

In this manner, he followed the trail for several miles, finally stopping to make a cold camp on a small bluff above the Cucharas River.

He was on the trail again at first light. It had curved in an arc to the northeast, following the river on its course to the Arkansas. Tate thought the outlaws might be headed toward Albert Boone's spread, a hacienda located at the junction of the Arkansas and Cucharas Rivers, built by the grandson of the legendary trailbreaker, Daniel Boone. Yet, he surmised that Vivian was severely wounded and losing much blood. It was more likely that they would hold up for a few days somewhere on the prairie, then push west toward the Huerfano Valley and on to the village of Pueblo. If Vivian could travel, they might even cross into the southern gold camps.

Finally, the trail was completely gone. Several days and the magnificent storm had rearranged the land, smoothing it with wind and water. In addition, the outlaws had probably slowed their flight, taking care to cover their tracks.

It was now that Tate's tracking ability was at its finest. For 35 years, friends and enemies alike had expressed wonder at Tate's skill at both breaking new trails and following old ones. It was noted countless times that he could out track a bloodhound. Even the U.S. Army retained him for their most difficult job, tracking Apache warriors, the finest guerrilla soldiers in the world, through the Arizona desert. He confounded his companions, tracking both man and beast quicker and more accurately than any of the other rough frontiersmen. His was a valuable ability, and he honed it into an art.

He had told no one save Carson that the ability to track transcended the physical. Tate operated in that zone saved for those who are the best at any endeavor. He relied on his intuition. More often than not, he could visualize the probable actions of those he followed, especially if they were men on the run. He often rationalized this ability as plain old common sense, but he knew it transcended any such simple platitude. His was a harsh world, filled with harsh personalities. He learned young to identify the causes and effects that motivated people in such a severe environment. He learned to listen. He learned to watch. He saw cruel actions, and observed that those who perpetrated such cruelty were generally alike in attitude and personality. They tended to act similarly, reacting to their exacting environments rather than managing them. They lived in the present and seldom planned anything beyond their next meal. Even when premeditated, their crimes were haphazard. He learned to know such men, and when he was younger even fought the urge to become one of them.

He took little pride in his ability to crawl inside an outlaw's head. In fact, he was disturbed and perhaps even ashamed by the capacity, judging it to be a character defect. Each time he allowed himself to intuitively deduce the actions of one of society's predators, he felt like a drunkard who had sworn off rotgut, but always craved its taste. He was soothed only in that his conscience, when he allowed himself to examine it and travel its distant borders, allowed him few regrets. He had followed the laws of life instilled in him by his father in St. Louis so long ago, and they had served him well.

Now, he sat lightly in the saddle on the bluffs above the Cucharas River and studied the soggy landscape. Knowing that the trail was cold, he allowed himself to enter the realm of intuition, surmising the probable area where the outlaws would have had to stop to make camp and tend to the wounded killer, Vivian Garcia. He knew they could not have traveled much more than 20 miles from Herold's Crossing without leaving the oldest bandido a rotting corpse on the prairie.

Tate rode about a mile from the river on the east side, zigzagging back and forth, judging angles, separating the land into quadrants to be searched. Late in the afternoon, his eyes fell on a thicket of pinons leading down the slope of a small arroyo. A tiny brook bubbled out of the depression. As he approached, he saw two impressions of horses' hooves, the tracks of one of horses he had been following. Apparently, one of the outlaws, most likely Filipio, had been scouting the area, looking for pursuit.

Tate dismounted and picketed his horse to a small willow downstream from the arroyo. Unsheathing both rifles, he began a slow, sure approach to the gully. His moccasins were silent on the land, and he moved like a ghost in the impending twilight. He approached slowly, in a crouch, taking advantage of every opportunity to stop in shadows and study the gulch. Finally, he circled around to the top of the rise where the cleft in the earth began and waited once more. Seeing the tops of a small grove of willows that grew in the gap, he stopped and listened intently. The sounds of magpies and finches were all he heard, and he knew from their chatterings that the arroyo was empty.

Still, he moved cautiously down the eastern slope of the depression, entering the bottom in a small grassy area where horses had obviously been picketed for some days. He scanned the area where the outlaws had camped. Something caught his eye, and he reached over and picked up a blood-soaked strip of cloth.

So, Vivian was still alive. And still bleeding.

He searched the ground for other telltale signs of the group, but found nothing save the depressions where two men slept, and one man leaned against a saddle.

He ambled down the arroyo, following sign that indicated the departure of the bandits. Suddenly he stopped, his heart pounding. The tracks led upward, out of the arroyo on the west side, not toward Boone's hacienda or Pueblo, but back south along the west bank of the Cucharas River. The realization of what the outlaws planned came over him, and he spoke aloud.

"Aiyeee," he said in a guttural drawl. "Divil's threw me fer a loop awright."

He quickly followed the tracks to the top of the slope and looked back to the southwest.

"Damn, they's backtrackin'. Jake and his lads had best be on lookout. Them soulless pigs're headed back."

*"The coyote stood... looking
hungrily at him."*

CHAPTER SIX

LIBBY HEROLD WAS ELATED. The supply wagons that had cut
north from the Santa Fe Trail arrived the day before, bearing not only the essentials necessary to operate a trading
post, but items that reminded her that civilization did
indeed exist somewhere to the east. Four gingham dresses
she ordered from an Independence tailor arrived and had
alrcady been tried on and modeled before the critical eyes
of her family. Stephen and John had been appreciative, and
Jake had beamed before giving her a peck on the cheek
and going outside the family quarters to settle up with the
traders. Only young Amos was reserved, refraining from
the effusive praise his mother had received from the family's other men. He had yet to fully develop the art of flat-
tery, and preferred his mother in one of her homemade
broadcloth dresses, or even the man's shirt and trousers
she infrequently wore when planting and tending the
family's garden.

Libby had noted her youngest son's reticence with
amusement, wryly pondering the introspection boys must
endure when realizing that their mothers are also women,
who love women's things. Respecting Amos's discomfort,
she donned a faded blue broadcloth dress upon awaking.
Now, after breakfast, she sent Amos to the well for water

71

while Jake and the older boys tended to the livestock.

Libby began an inventory of the trading post's stock, integrating the newly-arrived food and merchandise with the present supplies. As she worked she allowed herself to reflect upon how lighthearted the arrival of the supply wagons had made her. Although the West was her home, she could not forget the tree lined lanes of Philadelphia, nor the marketplaces with their limitless wares.

The frontier was hard, indeed. It was particularly hard on women. Libby Herold was no exception. As a child, she had allowed her imagination to run wild, listening to stories of the Wild West. She never imagined she would some-day live that hard, yet ultimately rewarding life.

One of eight children born to a cooper and his wife, she had grown up around wood, loving its smell and textures. She often spent days in the working area, at her father's side as he cut stout oak boards to perfection before fitting them to forms and submerging them to allow the bending process to occur. She loved the ring of the hammer on the giant black anvil as strong iron hoops were formed. Most of all she loved the final products, barrels and casks that seemed more like fine furniture than receptacles.

Because her father's trade was brisk, she was given the opportunity to attend school, where she excelled. She always assumed that she would someday be a teacher, or at least the wife of a teacher. That was before a young man named Jake Herold rode up to her father's works in a wagon pulled by a double team. The horses were magnifi-cent, the result of noted breeding stock fostered by the Herold family. Jake tethered the team and walked inside the cooper's works to discuss ordering several oaken casks for the Herold farm. A few minutes later, from inside the adjacent house, sixteen-year-old Libby noticed the dou-ble team tied to a rail placed under a huge maple. She left the house and walked to the horses, running her hands through their groomed manes and talking to them softly.

72

She was so entranced with the steeds that she failed to notice a young man approach from her father's shop.

After listening to Libby talk nonsense to his team for a minute, Jake Herold quietly cleared his throat. Startled, Libby's hand flew to her mouth as she turned. Jake's bemused smile became a full-fledged grin as he saw the beautiful young girl before him.

Recovering quickly, Libby laughed and questioned him about the team. Herold leaned against the hitching rail and began to tell her about the complexities of raising horse-flesh. The conversation turned and twisted, and over the next half-hour, he was surprised to learn that young Libby Sykes was something he had not expected to find—a kindred spirit.

They talked of heroic exploits on the Western prairie and of stories relating the impossible heights of the Rocky Mountains. They talked about how confining Philadelphia was becoming, how it often seemed impossible to traverse the clogged streets. They talked of wanderlust and adventure.

When he reluctantly steered the wagon away from the coopersmith's, Jake Herold was in love for the first time in his nineteen years.

Over the next few months, Herold returned to the shop whenever he could convince his father and brothers that he needed to check on the progress of the casks that were being fashioned. His father assumed the young man had a reason for taking such deep interest in the cooper's trade, and he supposed correctly that it wore skirts. Not one to stifle impulses either romantic or adventurous in his children, he rarely questioned Jake's excuses for traveling the 12 miles to monitor cooper Sykes' work.

Wendell Sykes was renowned for the quality of his tubs and casks, and spent most of his time teaching his sons the intricacies of the trade. The trade of a cooper was man's work, and as much as he appreciated his daughter's interest in wood and smithing, he knew she was destined for other things—other people. Noticing the attention being given to Libby by Jake Herold, he absentmindedly pondered the possibilities inherent in such a match. Herold horseflesh in the family! Imagine!

Five months later, Libby and Jake were on a Sunday stroll on the grounds of a small Lutheran church when she impulsively grabbed the tall young man's hands, spun him around to her, looked searchingly into his eyes, and asked his intentions. He was both shocked and elated by her forwardness and told her so. She allowed that she may have been out of line, but that if their feelings were mutual, it merely seemed practical to tie the knot and get on with their lives. From that day on, Jake often noted that in his experience, he was the only man on the continent to have been roped and hog-tied while innocently walking on consecrated ground.

Following a small wedding, they moved to the Herold farm, where they occupied a tiny house built by Jake and his brothers. Jake raised horses, wheat, and hay while Libby raised both bread dough and Jake's spirits.

That first summer, they would walk out into the darkness after a late supper and lay back in the great mounds of hay, looking at the stars. They talked constantly, as young lovers do. Their curiosity about the untamed Western territories was unquenchable, and they intently discussed news of the frontier.

One day early the following spring, a bearded, deerskin-clad rider approached the Herolds' barn. The father and brothers noticed the unusual mare the man was riding, and that it was slightly hobbled.

"Heer'd you was horsemen," the rider said.

"You heard right, sir," answered the elder Herold. "But, I've not seen a horse such as this. Where did you get her?"

"Ketched 'er, lad," chuckled the man. "Out to the wild flats of Ute country."

Jake was delighted by the man's speech—a mixture of English, French, and Spanish with a dash of the high country Indian thrown in. As the others tended to the injured mare, Jake invited the man into the house for food and drink.

For the next few hours, Jake and Libby were entertained by fabulous stories from Simon LaBrie, who called himself a mountain man. He told them of John Colter's Hell, of the great lake in Ute country that was as salty as the sea, of monstrous grizzly bears and spectacular mountains. He told them of both savage and noble Indians and of gold for the taking.

Finally, he told them of the beauty of the land, and of his contention that civilization was spreading West, like it or not. He told them of a group of French Canadians who had settled in with the Spanish in southern New Mexico territory. The Spanish had been there for years, he said, but welcomed new neighbors. The land was fertile and water was plentiful, he said. In fact, he was heading back after taking care of some matters in Quebec.

He told them of the mountain man Sam Tate, and of his love for the Spanish Peaks. Should they ever decide the land that was now being called Colorado was for them, just see Tate, he said.

"Give yeer interductions to 'ol Samuel 'n tell 'im Bald Simon give ye directions," he chuckled, then pulled off his fur cap to display a grotesque scar running through the side of his thick hair. He had been scalped.

"Red divil skul'ped me a little too quick," he said, amusement in his voice. "Paid fer it, too."

For the next few months, Jake and Libby refrained from talking about the mountain man's visit. But often as not, they would end up at day's end looking toward magnificent sunsets out to the west. LaBrie's gruesome stories of conflict between white and red men aside, the couple still could not shake the growing certainty that their destiny lay at the foot of the great Western mountains. Over time, Jake's father noticed the wanderlust and finally sat the young couple down. The Pennsylvania economy was less than robust, and he knew he must plan for his children the best way he could. Should Jake and Libby choose to emigrate West, he thought, it would leave Jake's brothers in that much better position to contend with the arduous life of the farm.

When they were finished talking, the elder Herold had promised six prime horses should the couple decide to follow their dreams to the West.

Jake would not allow himself to order Libby to enter this life of hardship and uncertainty. They discussed it for hours, and finally he told her the decision was hers.

Libby was forced at last to face the reality of moving across an entire continent to wild country she neither knew nor could even really imagine. She would leave virtually everything, including her family. It took her an anguished week to come to terms with the fact that Jake would wither on the vine if they stayed, and become old before his time. She also knew that their world was shrinking, and that their dreams lay where they always had—to the West, in what were now being called the Rocky Mountains. She began packing without telling him of her decision, savoring the surprise in his eyes as he walked into their house and saw the trunks and cases scattered about.

Jake immediately went to work putting together a group of adventurous souls, counting on strength in numbers to ensure a safe journey through a savage country. Eventually, 11 families and 24 single men banded together, leaving Philadelphia in the spring of 1847.

They were pioneers.

At Independence, Missouri, the group split into two parties. Most of the families wanted to continue on to California via the northern trail to Oregon. An emotional parting followed, and Jake and Libby joined 18 people from their group as well as 35 people from assorted other bands on the southern trek along the Santa Fe Trail.

The group hired a scout named Jim Tatum who had been recommended as a competent frontiersman. How competent they didn't know until a Comanche raiding party halted their progress near Fort Dodge. Tatum engaged the Indians in a conversation and trading session, which he termed a "dam-gummed powwow," and success-fully negotiated their safe passage to Santa Fe. Jake spoke to Tatum about the advisability of striking due west from Fort Dodge along the Arkansas River which would bring his outfit close to the Spanish Peaks he sought. Tatum let on that if Jake and Libby reached Bent's Trading House, they would likely be all right, but the prospects of that happening were about the same as a rattler singing "Barbara Allen."

The Herolds continued with the others along the Santa Fe Trail until they were in the shadow of the mountains. Tatum told them they would likely be safe heading due north to the Spanish Peaks, traveling through the predom-inantly Spanish settlements. He drew a crude map of the *haciendas* they would pass on their way to a river called the *Cucharas*.

Now, taking inventory in her store these 18 years later, Libby reflected on the time that had passed. In an instant she reviewed the kindness of Sam and Esther Tate, the encouragement of John Francisco, and the friendship of Emily Gorner. She remembered first laying her eyes on the spread the Herrera family offered to let them buy, and the delight she found in the grove of cottonwoods and wil-lows that covered the bend in the river.

Their sons were born here. First Stephen, a year after Jake and several *vaqueros* from neighboring ranches had erected their first small house, a cabin really. John was born two years later, when Jake had made the decision to

77

add cattle to their property and, at the same time, open a small trading post to serve the people of the valley. Finally, Amos was born one night when a gorgeous, silky summer moon rose over the west peak of the *Huajatolla,* illuminating the Herold's hacienda-style house and trading post.

They had seen their dream grow. They had survived hardship and struggle. They had learned the power of love, the power of family, and the power of community. They never regretted their decision to head West for one minute.

Her reverie was interrupted when she heard Herold's bootsteps on the short boardwalk in front of the trading house. She turned to greet him as he walked through the door and watched him remove his broadbrimmed hat and toss it on a folded horse blanket.

"So, you're tuckered out already?" she teased.

"Yep," he answered, "can't take any more. Sun's too hot and I'm too old. Thought I'd just sit around in here and watch you for a day or two."

"You'll be watching a regular Kansas twister, Mr. Jake Herold," she said, chuckling. "This is about to become the cleanest trading post in Colorado territory."

Herold laughed as he crossed the room to a water pitcher. He poured a glass.

"Amos is fetching fresh water, if you want to wait a short spell," Libby said.

Herold sipped the brackish water, winced and said, "Don't mind if I do. This tastes like three-day-old coffee."

Jake sat on a high-backed wooden chair, a relic of their days in Pennsylvania. He picked up a brown canvas bag and fiddled with it. It contained correspondence from back East that had made its way along the Santa Fe Trail. The Eastern immigrants along the Cucharas were waiting to hear the news from whence they came.

"Believe I'll ride on out this afternoon and deliver letters," he said.

"Now that the war's over, it'll take a while to shake out all that's happened. I 'spect there's both good and bad news to be delivered."

The previous April had been the most momentous in the young nation's history, and those in the West waited with near unendurable anxiety for news. Copies of Eastern papers chronicling the negotiations between Grant and Lee at Appomattox made their way across the great Western trails and were devoured by news-hungry pioneers. The weeping in Denver and Fort Dodge at news of President Lincoln's assassination was equally intense as anywhere in the wounded nation.

The Civil War had been hard on everyone, Westerners included. Jake's brother Charles had died in the battle of Nashville while another brother, Elam, had been grievously wounded on Cemetery Ridge at Gettysburg. Libby had lost her youngest brother, Billy, at the prisoner of war camp at Andersonville. Details were sketchy, but like thousands of others, he likely died of dysentery.

The Southern pioneers who had settled near Huerfano Butte were equally affected. Kate and Martha Patterson had long conversations with Herold about the causes and effects of the war. Although in sympathy with the South, they were now Westerners, and the sting of the war half a continent away was lessened by the high plains and towering peaks of the West. They would not allow themselves to divide the fledgling community along ideological lines. Other Southern thugs had tried that approach, and the Army of the Missouri had dealt with them effectively.

Patterson and the Russell brothers, Green, Levi, and Oliver, decided to return to Georgia as soon as possible to check on their families. They prepared themselves for the worst, yet knew they had to bring survivors west to the Spanish Peaks country.

Herold also felt the need to travel east, to view the devastation he was spared and to lay eyes on his and Libby's surviving family. Libby agreed, and Herold planned to leave for Pennsylvania following the harvest. He would travel with the Georgians along the Santa Fe Trail back to Independence before breaking off and heading northeast. She and the boys would remain, with young Jim Patterson staying at the Crossing for added protection.

Sitting in his chair at his trading post on the Cucharas, Herold thought that the harvest seemed a long way off, indeed. Two months at least. So much had happened recently, including the Gorners' murders, that he felt insecure about leaving. In his mind, he knew he wouldn't go if the Garcias were still at large.

"Lib, I been thinking hard for the past couple of days. I need to do something about this Garcia business. I know Sam's out on their trail, and I expect they'll be wolf meat before long."

A long, drawn out sigh escaped him before he continued. "But I can't forget about Emily, what they did to her. Or what they tried to do to us. I need to help."

Libby turned toward Herold, not speaking. She knew it was a time to listen.

"Sam told John Francisco and me that Kit was sendin' Homer Keating and a couple of Ute scouts up the Huerfano. They'll be stopping here sometime today or tomorrow before breaking off. I think Billy Carson should be at Fort Francisco by tomorrow. Kate'll be there, too. I've decided to go in and hook up with Billy 'n Kate, convince 'em to track the middle ground between the two rivers. Some of us are bound to run across those animals."

Libby crossed the room to her husband, knelt and held his hands in hers. She stared into the light of the doorway for a moment, then spoke.

"Jake, I know you have to go. But I couldn't bear the thought of not seeing you again."

A single tear ran down her cheek, splashing on the scuffed wood floor. She sniffed lightly and continued.

"You know the ways of this country as well as any man, I know that. But," she paused and looked directly at Herold, "I think these men are more vicious than any you've faced before. They'll lay traps, Jake. They'll ambush anyone. They're fanatics. Sam told us so. The one Amos shot thinks he's God or something."

"I know, Lib," Jake said. "I know. But he's *not* God, and he's gotta pay. Billy's been taught by his papa and Sam— he's one of the best outdoorsmen in these parts. And between Kate and me, well, you know we've tracked down our share of bad men."

Libby nodded, knowing now there was no dissuading him. Yet she couldn't help trying.

"Couldn't you at least hook up with the trooper from Fort Garland? Homer Keating? Wouldn't it give you all more protection?"

"That it would," he answered. "But it would also weaken the net, give 'em a better chance to get through.

"No, Kate 'n Billy 'n me'll make a fine group. If we all spread out, Sam on one side, Homer on the other and us in the middle, I know we'll get 'em. We'll *get* 'em, Libby."

Libby's body was wracked with a huge sigh. Finally, she shook her head in agreement and lay it against Herold's knee.

"Yes, Jake, get them. I miss Emily so. I can't even get it through my mind that she's really gone. And that poor little angel, Johnny. He was such a Gorner, just like his papa. I don't..."

The cracks of three nearby rifle shots pierced the air. Herold was up and running for the door, grabbing his double-barreled shotgun, before Libby could stand. She saw him fly out the door as she began to run herself, her heart caught in her throat.

John Herold had mischief on his mind. After the somber

introspection of the last few days in reaction to the deaths of the Gorners, he was ready to once again join the world by demonstrating a young man's ebullience. John had always been the liveliest of the three brothers, playing practical jokes on friends and family and generally bringing smiles to the faces inhabiting the Cucharas Valley. The Gorner murders had dampened that enthusiasm. John thought the world of his young namesake, John Gorner, and seeing the boy lying in the dirt, his lifeblood being soaked up by the thirsty earth, had thrown him into shock. John had lifted the young boy's body and carried it into the shed where Emily's body had already been covered by his father. He had cried over the young boy, and gently closed his eyes. He refused to change his own bloodstained clothes after the Herolds had returned to the Crossing, and only did so after Stephen slapped him back to reality.

The Gorner funeral had been agonizing. Seeing the coffins of his neighbors and friends being committed to the earth had not offered any solace. Rather, it had only increased his grief and anger.

Afterward, his mother calmly put her arm around his shoulders and led him off to a field of wild daisies growing near the gravesite. They stood looking out over the Colorado foothills, and she spoke to him soothingly, telling him about the mysterious journey that was life, and how shock and dismay were as natural as joy and elation. He clung to his mother and cried for nearly ten minutes, exorcising the demons he had contained within. He never loved her more than at that moment.

Now, as he watched his little brother Amos leave the family's living quarters with the five gallon water bucket in his hand, John decided a little fun was in order. Life was beginning to seem as if it were for living once again.

Amos stepped off the boardwalk, rounded the corner of the trading post, and headed for the well thirty yards to the side of the building. He stopped briefly to put down the bucket, hitch up his hand-me-down trousers around his waist, and continue his task. With Amos's back turned to the corral, it was simple for John to take off in the underbrush and willows, and to circle through the dense foliage toward the deep well where Amos was headed.

The Herold boys had always been encouraged by their father to "play Indian," learning to sneak silently through the underbrush, concealing their movements and observing their quarry. On the hard Western frontier, it was never known when such talents would become necessary.

The well was in the open, between the trading post structure and a 40 yard-long wall of wild blueberry bushes that gradually fused into a near-impassable thicket. Over the years, John and Stephen had hacked a low passage through the bushes, often hiding in the retreat to fantasize about tracking Indians and battling outlaws. John followed the well-worn track through the bushes now, intending to spring from the bushes and scare Amos out of his wits. Stephen, the oldest, had done the same to John, and now Amos stood next in line.

Parting the dense bushes, John saw Amos standing at the well, preparing to lower the bucket into the cool water. John crept silently along the passage and primed himself to scare his brother by screaming like a banshee from hell. He slowly knelt and took in a huge breath.

Just then, he heard the soft neigh of a nearby horse. Startled, he dropped to the ground, counted to ten to still his heart and then slowly lifted his head, peering through the dense vegetation. At first he saw nothing. Then, as his eyes began to discern between the countless points of light and darkness in the thicket, a perfectly camouflaged dun stallion standing 20 yards away came into view. The saddle seemed new, incongruent with the worn rigging, and the horse appeared exhausted, although he could not be sure. John moved slightly to his right to get a better look at the horse. It was then that he noticed a deep wound in its flank, crusted over and starting to heal. He felt the bile rise in his throat as he realized that the horse, that particular horse, was not tied to a branch for lack of a reason.

As he prepared to back up and scoot along the passage to get his father, he noticed another movement. A black sombrero on the other side of the horse moved slowly around to the animal's rear. The hat's owner came into view, moving slowly. The man was obviously in great pain, his breathing labored. He stopped behind the horse, then moved off to its right, leaning against a slim cottonwood growing in the midst of the thicket. His filthy clothes were soaked with sweat, and he inhaled great gulps of air. Slowly, he removed a pistol from a black holster around his waist and gingerly transferred it to his left hand. He winced and took another ragged breath before extracting bullets from a *bandolero* and slowly loading the gun.

Vivian Garcia! John could hardly keep the name inside his mouth. So, the outlaw was alive and had come back to Herold's Crossing. The others had to be near, then, John reasoned.

He forced himself to be calm and slowly turned and backed up through the passage. He looked back toward the well and saw Amos dallying, playing with the rope tied to the bucket now deep in the cold water. He could hear Amos humming a familiar song, oblivious to any danger.

John held his breath and moved slowly, imperceptibly through the foliage. When he thought he was far enough from the outlaw, he raised himself on all fours and quickly crawled through the remainder of the branch-infested tunnel.

He had left his rifle near the gatepost of a corral where he was tending to the dozen heifers being raised by the family, and now saw it ahead. He emerged from the thicket and sprinted toward the rifle, only to see a dark form emerge from the trees to his left. He leapt toward the rifle and grabbed it, rolling into a fence post and stopping. He saw the figure raise its rifle at the same time as he brought his to play. John felt a bullet splat in front of his outstretched leg before he squeezed off two quick shots, grazing the figure and forcing it back into the trees. As John processed this information, he realized that the figure was in reality a boy, much smaller than him—*Santiago Garcia!*

John kept the rifle aimed in the general area where the man had disappeared, knowing that his father and Stephen would be hurrying out to help. He quickly turned toward the well and saw Amos transfixed as another form shot out from the thicket. Filipio Garcia ran toward Amos, his pistol unholstered. The boy snapped out of his trance and tried to move backward, but the outlaw was upon him, tackling him. At the same time, Jake Herold came bursting around the side of the building, his shotgun cocked and ready. Both Herold and John had their guns covering the outlaw, who now stood with Amos held hostage before him. Quickly, the *pistolero* backed up toward the thicket, his forearm around the boy's neck. As he reached the edge of the vegetation, he threw Amos into the foliage, squeezed off two shots in the vicinity of Herold's position, and disappeared.

"Dad! They're *all* there, back in the weeds," screamed John. Herold quickly ran toward the well and rolled behind a nearby water trough.

"Johnny, take cover!" he yelled and watched his son scamper behind a cattle feed box near the corral. As John moved, the boy Santiago fired from behind his position at the perimeter of the thicket. John's boot heel went flying, landing in the clearing several feet away. He inspected his foot, then waved at his father to indicate he had not been hit.

"Steve? You there?" yelled Herold.

No answer.

85

"Steve!" he bellowed. As he fought down the panic that came from one son's capture and another's silence, Herold looked behind him, to the clearing in front of the trading house. He glimpsed Stephen's bright red shirt as the boy dove for cover behind an ox-wagon. At least Stephen was all right. He also saw the hem of Libby's skirt protruding from around the corner, as well as the lowered barrel of his own Henry rifle.

Just then, Herold noticed more movement to the rear. Three men dressed in navy blue cavalry shirts, two Indian and one white, were fanning out toward the edge of the thicket. Jake recognized Homer Keating from the soldier's many stops at the crossing. He assumed the Indians were the Ute scouts Tate had mentioned.

So, they had a small army to tackle the vermin hiding in the thicket, Herold thought. It was small consolation, but welcome nonetheless.

Now, how to free Amos?

Keating quickly made his way to a position near the corner of the trading house. Spotting Herold, he quietly called out.

"They all in that passel 'a berry bushes, Jake?"

"Yep," responded Herold. "They got my youngest boy."

"Bobby 'n Ree'll take 'em from behind, Jake," the soldier said, indicating the two Indian scouts now on the move. Herold paused and looked completely around, trying to find some way to enter the maze. Finally, he spotted an opening, actually the exit to the passage created by John and Stephen.

Speaking only loud enough to be heard by John and Keating, he said, "Cover me, boys, I'm goin' in after 'em."

Before either could protest, Herold was dashing across the clearing to the thicket, rolling across the dry ground, leaving puffs of dust in the air. No shots were fired, which perplexed him. He rolled to the entrance of the thicket and lay still for a long moment. Then, he entered.

Vivian Garcia was livid. He wondered for a moment about which was worse, his anger or his pain. Unaware that he had been spotted by John Herold, who had gone to sound the alarm, he reasoned that Santiago must have taken a shot at someone. The damned kid had been nothing but trouble, he thought to himself. Now, he had alerted Herold and his sons. Luckily, Filipio had grabbed the young Herold boy.

Spotting his brother and the hostage through the thick foliage, Vivian used hand signals to indicate a retreat. They would have to take off and hole up for a few days, he reasoned, before returning and taking his revenge on Jake Herold. All the better, really, he thought. He needed more time to heal, to be able to move quickly and forcefully, as the Virgin had commanded.

Grabbing the reins of his mount, he quickly backed through the dense vegetation until he reached the horses of the other two outlaws, tied to small saplings in a clearing at the far side of the thicket. He saw Filipio coming toward them through the clearing with the Herold boy, now fighting and kicking. *Where was Santiago?* Suddenly, he saw a flash of dark blue in the trees behind Filipio and the boy. Before his could squeeze off a shot, a knife darted through the air and buried itself in the back of Filipio's left arm. The outlaw screamed and roughly tossed Amos Herold to the ground at the same time Vivian loosed two shots in the direction of the assailant. He saw a flash of long, black hair and high cheekbones, and realized with dread that an army scout had wounded his brother—an Indian. So, word of Tate's daughter's fate must have reached Carson. Now, the army had caught up with them. *Aiee,* he thought, *Filipio was right.* They should have gone north to the gold fields.

Near panic, Vivian agonizingly leaped on his horse and

viciously spurred it, forcing it into an immediate gallop. The pain of his wound made him woozy and unable to fully control the horse. As he tried to rein the stallion to the right to avoid a stout cottonwood, Jake Herold scrambled through the bushes and stepped directly into the horse's path. The trader brought the shotgun to bear on the fleeing desperado. Trying to control the horse with his wounded left arm, Vivian lifted the pistol in his right hand and tried to aim it toward Herold. Realizing he was about to be shot, he roughly yanked his stallion's reins straight back, causing the horse to rear at the same time Herold emptied the shotgun.

The dun stallion took the brunt of the assault, its neck turning bright red as the buckshot sliced through flesh, killing it instantly. Vivian was thrown from the horse as it went down, landing on his side and rolling to his left. The shock of the impact numbed his wounded shoulder temporarily and allowed him to quickly stand. Jake Herold was shoving two shells into the shotgun's double barrels. As he snapped the assembly together and began raising the weapon, Garcia swiftly brought his pistol up and fired. Herold was spun around by the impact of the bullet striking the left side of his body. He hit the ground hard just as a second bullet grazed his temple. He knew he had been hit, but couldn't feel the wound. He struggled to roll and come up off the ground to defend himself, but realized that the shotgun had fallen away. He attempted to get his bearings, fighting through the confusion and helplessness he felt. He heard a deafening report from behind him, then looked up from the ground only to see the outlaw standing next to the dead horse.

As Jake Herold drifted into unconsciousness, he wondered how Garcia could continue to stand with a fist-sized hole through his chest.

Vivian Garcia saw the coyote approaching. The slobbering, starving dog cowered a few feet away, its tail between its legs. A scorpion crawled along the animal's back, causing the fur to rise and fall along the vermin's path. Flies buzzed around its head, landing in the open, maggot-infested wounds that dotted its mangy body.

Garcia was confused. He remembered seeing the grizzled, bluecoated soldier part his way through the bushes behind Herold. He remembered the horrendous sound of the buffalo gun and the fire of the bullet penetrating his body. Then, he suddenly was standing in the familiar desert, his wounds healed. The smells of gunpowder and sweat were replaced by those of blooming cactus and dry desert wind.

Walking away from the disgusting coyote, he found he was headed toward the chapel in the distance. Its cross stood out against the whitewashed adobe. The cool mountains in the background beckoned.

He walked and walked. Hours passed, yet the chapel grew no closer. It remained within his vision, yet out of his reach.

He looked around questioningly and saw his tracks leading back into the distance, into an infinite desert. Each of the footprints was on fire, sending thousands of small plumes of smoke up into the crystal clear air. The coyote stood several feet away, looking hungrily at Garcia. It began to whine.

Suddenly, Vivian was very tired. He lay down in the hot sand, closed his eyes and felt the sun warm his face.

A shadow passed over and stinking drool splattered onto his face. He opened his eyes and saw the putrefying coyote standing above him, wheezing obscenely.

He tried to raise his arm to scare the animal away, but he had no strength left. It stood above him, its head moving in a semicircular motion from side to side, as if questioning something.

"Go, coyote," he said weakly. "I rest here before meeting the Virgin. She will come to me."

The panting coyote circled the outlaw three times, then carefully climbed onto his chest. Exhaustion encompassed Garcia, making him powerless to shake the repulsive coyote off as it lowered its muzzle to his face. Their noses touched and Vivian looked directly into the scavenger's eyes. They seemed bottomless, extending beyond the stars. Impossibly deep within were miniature suns, each beating down with incredible heat into the killer's very soul. The dog let loose a high, whining growl. Then, to Vivian's horror, it spoke.

"No, Vivian," whispered the coyote in a jester's voice, his stinking breath gagging the prostrate outlaw. "The Virgin will *not* come. We follow another path together, you and I."

Vivian Garcia lay paralyzed with both fear and revulsion. In that scorching, forever desert, he was denied even the release of screaming.

"...Libby leaned her back against a crossrail and gazed off toward the Huajatolla."

CHAPTER SEVEN

"THEY TOOK THE BOY, SAM."

Homer Keating leaned against the interior pine wall of the trading house at Herold's Crossing. The firelight from the pinon fire danced across his weathered, mustached face, giving him the look of an ancient Saxon chieftain.

Sam Tate had appeared out of the darkness minutes before, stealing up to the house after scouting the corral and recognizing Keating's roan mare. He hailed the house, and heard Keating and Stephen Herold answer simultaneously.

Keating wasted no time in telling him about the battle with the Garcias that afternoon.

"Afore Vivian joined them demons in Hell, he managed to put a .45 clean through Jake. Nicked him on the haid, too. Miz Herold's with 'im now. It's a dangerous hole was opened, but he'll not go under. Jake's a strong'un, awright."

Tate narrowed his eyes and nodded.

"That he is, Homer. It's shameful sech a good'un had to get shot up by..." He paused for a moment, holding the profanity and pulling his anger under control. After a short silence, he continued.

"So, Vivian's gone under?"

"Yep," answered Keating. "I pulled my Sharps out without much thinkin' when we heered the gunfire on over the ridge. Primed 'er then and there. Carried 'er through yonder thicket after Jake'd gone on through. Found the divil ready to finish Jake off. Jake'd spent his shells—kilt Vivian's dun pony.

"I kilt Vivian," he said, matter-of-factly.

"Mighty queersome, it was. I seen men hit with buffler guns afore, fallin' to the ground and floppin' like catfish on the shore. This divil just stood up like a damn griz for the longest time afore crumblin' over on that dead hoss. Damn! His heart was shot out."

Tate absorbed the image, taking some small pleasure in the thought of Garcia standing there, wondering what happened as his life drained away.

"How'd the other divils escape ye?" asked Tate.

"Readin' they sign, looks like they jist took off whilst Jake 'n Vivian was shootin' it out. Bobby here seen the young 'un scat afore the shootin' even started. After Vivian went down, I seen Filipio was a-horseback 'bout a hunderd yards out, holdin' Herold's boy he was, an' goin' over a bluff afore we could get a shot off. Bobby 'n me tried to foller, but they pinned us down in a gully 'bout a mile north.

"We was one short, cause Ree was back here nursin' a nasty hole in his arm he took from ol' Vivian. He managed to bury one'a them throwin' knives he carries in Filipio's arm first, though.

"After it got dark, I sent Bobby out to circle 'em where they holed up, while I kep' firin' above they heads ever' few minutes. Pretty soon, Bobby lets loose with a whoop an' shoots onct in the air. I caught up with him shortly 'n saw where them outlaws had took out to the southwest, headed toward the Saddle, looks like. Wadn't nothin' we could do to track 'em tonight, so we came back here to tend to Jake 'n the others. We'll head out after 'em in the mornin'.

"Sam, I told ye they took young Amos. There's no sign of him where they holed up. All we found was the knife that'd been stickin' outta Filipio's arm."

Stressing the obvious, Keating said, "I just wish ol' Ree'd a put that knife through his evil heart, instead."

Tate shook his head in agreement and stroked his stubbled chin.

"Mighty fateful ye showed up when ye did," he said.

"Yep," answered Keating. "We was headed up the Huerfano, like you 'n Kit 'n me planned at the Fort. Planned to stop in here fust fer any fresh news.

"Still cain't ken what brought them divils back through these parts."

"Hard to figger sometimes," said Tate. "I felt foolish as a young pup when I found their camp up near the Arkansaw and figured what they was up to. I thought I'd be trailin' 'em up Cripple Crick way by now.

"Damn near killed 'ol Tom spurrin' 'im back here."

Tate sat back and took stock of his surroundings for the first time since he arrived. In addition to the hearth fire, three oil lamps were lit about the room. John and Stephen Herold sat near the doorway to the family's living quarters. Each cradled a rifle and took in Keating's report to Tate with rapt attention.

Following their brother's abduction, they had begun to saddle up and follow the outlaws despite Keating's objections. Their father was unconscious, their brother stolen, and their lives seemed to be shattered. Action was called for, and a manhunt was the only action they could imagine.

As they feverishly prepared their pursuit, Libby appeared from the trading post and called them into the building. They followed her into the room where they had carried their father and where he now lay unconscious.

They were shocked by her appearance. In the past few hours, she seemed to have grown haggard from worry and fear. Her hair hung in untidy strands over the collar of her soiled dress, and they noticed crow's feet around her eyes for the first time.

"Steve, Johnny," she said stiffly. "I've almost lost your father today. I may have lost your brother."

She turned and looked earnestly at her two oldest sons and spoke vehemently in a staccato cadence. *"I will not lose you!"*

The brothers were shocked by their mother's intensity. They had never seen her speak so forcefully. Yet, still they began to protest, excitedly jabbering about the need to follow the outlaws, to rescue Amos.

"Enough!" she screamed.

The young men were reduced to dead silence. They saw the single tear make its way down their mother's cheek, and saw her fight to control the trembling that had overtaken her body.

"I've spoken with Mr. Keating, who has put forth a serviceable plan."

Libby quietly moved to a bent rocker in the corner of the room, where she sat and collected herself. She put her hands to her face, aware that her sons were absorbed by her every move.

"It will do absolutely no good for either of you to go chasing after the vermin who have Amos. You come from different lives, different worlds, really.

"Now, Mr. Keating and his scouts will follow the trail and try to free Amos. It will be dark soon, so he is not sure that much can be accomplished. But at least he is familiar with these people. He can think like them, which is something neither of you can."

Another tear made its way down her cheek, followed by its twin down the other. She took several racking breaths and said, "As God is my witness, I know he will catch them. I know he will bring Amos home.

"I need you here now. If Mr. Keating weren't here, and if Mr. Tate and Mr. Carson and Mr. Patterson were not also involved in the chase, it would be a different story. But for now, we need to nurse your father, and you need to run the spread."

The brothers fought to keep their emotions in check, forcing themselves to the realization that their mother was right. Yet, the urge for revenge was powerful, and the anxiety concerning Amos stronger still.

Both walked to their mother, leaned over and kissed her wet cheeks. She hugged them with astonishing strength, letting them go only after she intuitively felt they would obey her.

"Let's go out and help Mr. Keating plan—let your father rest," she said. They quietly left the room, closing the door on a barely conscious Jake Herold, who had heard the exchange through the hot mist of pain and crude sedatives and marveled at the woman who was his wife.

Later, when Keating returned with news that the outlaws were likely spurring their horses toward the saddle of La Veta Pass, Libby felt she had made the right decision. When she heard Sam Tate hail the house, she was sure of it. Tate would follow the Garcias to the ends of the earth, if necessary, and if Amos was to be saved, Sam Tate was the man to do it.

Libby sat in a Pennsylvania oak chair and listened through the door as Keating appraised Tate of the situation. She knew Sam Tate well, and knew that he was planning and scheming underneath the impassive exterior. She felt a strange calm, as if she and her family had passed some test, and the Lord had sent an avenging angel to right their wrongs.

In the next room, Tate pulled his pipe from his possibles sack, packed it with tobacco, and lit it with a quick flick of the wrist that, for him, served as a flourish. He puffed a few times, then looked at the Herold boys attentively waiting across the room.

"Now, Johnny lad, tell me the whole story from yer eyes. Then I'll want to hear what you have to say, Steve. Don't leave nothin' out. Tell me 'bout the hairs on the back 'a them divils' hands. Tell me 'bout the look in they eyes and the stink 'a they breath. Tell me the nicks on they guns, 'n the size 'a they hosses. Tell me everythin' lads, everythin'."

"Yessir," said John. "I don't know how it really happened, but I was followin' Amos out to the well, thought I might put a little scare into him..."

It took the Herold brothers nearly two hours to relate the events of the fight at Herold's Crossing. They told of John discovering Vivian Garcia and of his own shootout with Santiago Garcia. They told of Filipio Garcia's rough kidnapping of their brother. They told of pushing through the thicket in time to see Homer Keating shoot Vivian Garcia. They told of tending the scout Ree's flesh wound. Their stories were punctuated by questions from Tate, until every moment of the events was examined and digested by the mountain man.

When they were finished, Keating stood by the door with a shy grin on his weathered face. "Sam," he said, "I knowed ye was never one to let the wind pass by unnoticed, but these lads here got nothin' left. You took it all, hoss."

Tate allowed himself a small grin, his leathery face creasing at his forehead, crow's feet deepening at the corners of his eyes. He spoke once again to John and Stephen.

"Lads, this is important. We gotta know everythin' 'bout these divils—anythin' that might hep ketch 'em. You think of anythin' else, lemme know pronto.

"You done a fine job, lads. Yer pap 'n mam, well, they oughta be proud some, awright."

Tate was not one to hand out compliments, the brothers knew. The mountain man's praise had its intended effect of helping assuage the emotional devastation both felt after the long, eventful day.

Tate saw that the young men were clearly tired and almost giddy from the shock they had experienced. He glanced at Keating, indicating that they should talk alone outside.

"You pups best settle down fer the night," he said to John and Stephen. "Take care'a yer mam. Make sure she gets at least a little sleep.

"Homer and me, we'll take off yonder out by the willers 'n make camp. Check with ye in the dawn afore we set out to find yer brother."

The men stepped outside the structure and stood on the short boardwalk surrounding the store. Tate noticed the Ute scout Bobby standing in the shadows by the corner of the barn, keeping watch over his wounded companion, who sat upright against the wall. Keating nodded to the Utes and approached with Tate in tow. Speaking Spanish in low tones, they confirmed that Ree's wound was superficial, and that he was prepared to ride after the outlaws at first light.

Tate complimented the scout on his bravery and tenacity and, lost in thought, began walking toward the willow bank where he intended to camp. He stopped abruptly in a clearing halfway to the trees, and turned to Keating, who had been following closely.

"Homer, I got a feelin' I believe I'd best follow," he said. The old soldier returned his solemn look and nodded.

"Awright," said Keating, "let's hear it."

Tate mused for a few more seconds, then said, "It looks like them boys is headed up over the Saddle, awright. If'n they can get over the pass and skirt Fort Garland, make it on over to the Sand Mountains, they can head south through Antonito and Chama. Hell, I'll hafta tear half 'a the villages in the Sandias apart to find 'em. Now, they already got near half 'a day's start on us, and they'll be ridin' hard.

If Filipio knows anythin' 'bout the country, they won't make camp tonight. They'll just bust on through the gap, that is 'less Ree's throwin' knife did some mighty damage."

Keating raised his hand slightly, halting Tate.

"I don't know as much 'bout these boys as I do some others, hoss. Any chance they'll loop on back, try 'n collect ol' Vivian?"

Tate thought for a moment, then shook his head and answered.

"Naw, I 'spect Filipio'll jist let that 'ol moldering corpse be. I heerd tell that Filipio's nothin' but a murderin' dog. Puts no stock in killin' white folks for God. Kills 'em for hisself. I 'spect he thought Vivian's religion was just loco talk. No love lost between 'em. Nah, he prob'ly thinks sheddin' ol' Vivian was a fine idee."

Tate knelt and picked up a stick. The moonlight was bright enough to read by, and he dragged it through the dirt, drawing a crude map.

"Lemme show ye how I'm thinkin', Homer," he said as he began drawing landmarks in the dirt. He etched two vertical circles representing the *Huajatolla,* then a broad slash to the upper right. He added several small circles directly above the slash, and then added one long line leading left from the circles and two leading down from the slash.

Pointing to the slash, he said, "This here's La Veta Pass. Like I said, I think they's headed over to try to get to the Sand Mountains." Tate referred to the huge aggregate of sand dunes that lay mysteriously at the base of the Sangre de Cristo range west of Fort Garland.

He indicated the long line leading from the small circles. "Onct they're there, they kin either foller the Rio Grande here up on into the San Juans, or head south and come purty close to shakin' our trail. I cain't let that happen."

He moved the stick along the left side of the large

circles. "I think you 'n me both know they might take to skirtin' the whole mess and take off around the east Peak, head on down through the big pass at Raton and sneak on over to the Sandia country. They might, but I don't think they will. But we got to find out anyway."

He indicated the two long lines leading from the bottom of the map. "Only thing left fer 'em to do would be to foller the Cucharas or Huerfano out to the Arkansaw and try to hole up. I don't see 'em doin' that.

"Homer, I'm gonna head on after 'em 'n try to cut 'em off somewhere up on the pass. I don't believe I have time to foller their prints. I'm gonna hafta judge where they're headed. Meanwhile, mebbe you'n yer scouts can foller what tracks can be seen at dawn. If'n they look like they'll take off to the east of the Peaks, ye can foller 'n catch up. I 'spect their trail leads toward John Francisco's Fort. They'll veer off either west or south from there. I'm cuttin' across to the west, straight up the pass. I got the feelin' they'll keep in the tall timber. Not much up there, just a few rancher's 'n sech, so I should be able to sniff 'em out.

"Homer, ye head on through to Francisco's Fort and pick up them boys Jake said would be waitin' fer him. Ye knowed Billy Carson since he was a new pup. And Kate, he's fit to ride the trail with. They can spread out with ye lads, whether it be south or west."

Homer Keating studied the improvised map with an earnest eye, then stretched his long form until the bones in his shoulders cracked. Satisfied, he looked at Tate and said, "I ken yer plan, Sam. We'll do 'er, but I cain't have ye leavin' here tonight with no rest. Ye must catch yer wits, ol' hoss."

Tate stood slowly, his muscles aching from the long ride, and looked off into the darkness.

"Homer, that pig Filipio Garcia kilt my Emily. He kilt her good husband and her fine son and then he rutted with her like a pig in a sty afore chokin' her life away. I don't

101

rightly reckon I can sleep 'til his blood's on my hands. His 'n the young one's. Santiago's nothin' but a nit, and nits make lice.

"I was denied the righteous vengeance of killin' Vivian. Ye done that fer me. But the others, *they're mine!*"

He stopped suddenly, physically tearing himself away from the hate that engulfed him. He knew Keating was right, that he needed sleep. But he balanced that need with the urgency behind cutting off the flight. He knew full well that hate was not the only element that would fuel him. Amos Herold was in their hands, and as long as they had the boy, Tate could not afford to be reckless, to be overly bold. He could not allow his hate alone to spur him on. The boy's life depended on it.

He grabbed Keating's arm in his hand and squeezed. Looking back toward the trading house, he loosened his grip and patted the soldier's shoulder twice.

"Homer," he said, "I do need rest, awright. But I need sumpin' else worse. When I get a feelin', I got to go with it. Well, now I got a feelin'. I'm gonna walk back in an' talk to Miz Herold an' git her say to saddle up one 'a Jake's prize stallions here. Ol' Tom's near 'bout wore out 'n he needs a few days a high grass 'n sweet water, he does.

"Jake's hosses 're the best in the territory, so I'll have the advantage of a fine critter to ride into the timber. I've slept in the saddle afore, lad. So've ye, I suspect.

"Now ye 'n them trackers foller them divils at first dawn, hear?"

Keating nodded and smiled his sad smile. "Kit 'n me felt ye'd need little help, Sam. Prob'ly figgered right. But me 'n the boys, we'll be on the trail if'n ye're in need."

Tate brushed his foot through the crude map, then turned and walked toward the trading house. Halfway there, he furtively glanced behind him and saw Homer Keating standing ramrod straight, staring off toward the shimmering, still-snowcapped peaks of the *Huajatolla*, his ghostly form lit by the bright moon overhead.

After Tate had left, Libby Herold stationed her sons with her unconscious husband and slowly crossed the clearing toward the bank of willows. She had turned Jake's favorite stallion, Lancaster, over to Sam Tate, along with dried meat and supplies for his determined journey. Now, having sent her avenging angel on to his duty, she felt the need for confirmation, for consolation.

As she approached the willows, she softly called, "Mr. Keating? I wonder if we might speak?"

As if an apparition, Homer Keating materialized to her right, nearly startling her with his silence and grace. It was obvious that he had not been sleeping, but had been con- cealed in the shadows, waiting and watching. He approached her, making no sound on the soft soil. For the first time she noticed he wore calf-high moccasins instead of army issue boots.

"Yes'm," he said. "I spose ye've much on yer mind."

The frontiersman stood respectfully, his hat held in both hands before him. He slowly ran his right hand through his short-cropped hair and waited for Libby to speak.

"Perhaps we can walk while we talk, Mr. Keating," she said. "I feel the need to move, to be active."

She smiled wryly, then said, "It does seem that we try to walk away from our troubles, doesn't it?"

"Try as we might, ma'am, it just don't do much good," Keating answered.

The two walked slowly and silently for some yards, soaking in the moonlight that bathed the Herold spread. When they reached the corral, Libby leaned her back against a crossrail and gazed off toward the *Huajatolla*. Keating did the same.

"They're beautiful tonight," she said, nodding toward the twin peaks. "They're beautiful every night."

103

"That they are," said Keating. "Seems like I've knowed them peaks my whole life, but they look different ev'ry time I stare up at 'em. It's that way with mosta the mountain country, but these peaks do pull at somethin' inside ye, awright.

"Sam thinks they's spirits on the hills. Oh, not spirits like demons 'n sech, but spirits that tend to give ye a little courage when its necessary, that sorta thing."

Libby looked quickly away, and spoke into the night. "I do need such spirits now, Mr. Keating," she said, her eyes brimming with tears.

As she took a moment to compose herself, Keating looked at her with frank assessment. He was often amazed by the women of the frontier. They were as much pioneers as the men, he reckoned, and lived a much harder life in his opinion. Libby Herold, he saw, could rightly have been anything she wanted, a fine Eastern lady or perhaps a wealthy farmer's wife. Her broad, handsome features were made for the West, though, he thought. She and Jake were the kind of people he hoped would eventually follow when he first headed West all those years ago. Strong, principled people. He knew this land belonged to them now, and not to the trailblazers. His time was over, and he was ready to yield it graciously.

Finally, Libby broke the silence. "I need to know but one thing," she said. "Will Mr. Tate bring Amos home?"

Keating smiled benevolently, stroked his chin and answered, "Yes'm, I believe he will. Ain't no sech thing as a sure bet in this here world, ma'am. But if'n yer boy is to come back, I'd make a small wager Sam is the man to bring him.

"I might should tell you a story 'bout Sam Tate, Miz Herold. Some years back, over to the Arkansaw Valley, he found an empty settler's shack with a few arruhs stickin' out from it. The inside was tore to pieces. Unshod hoss tracks was everywhere about, so it wadn't hard to figger out the Kiowa was behind the whole mess. Settler's body was tied to a tree and—well, ye've heerd the stories, ma'am.

"Sam scouted 'round the place and found sign of a woman an' child. So, he figgers he'd best set off in search, see what the Kiowa had in mind. He followed them Indians upwards of a hunderd miles, up near the Republican River country. Found a war party of ten Kiowa holdin' the settler's wife and baby daughter. 'Course, knowing the Kiowa, Sam figgers they was to be slaves. So he comes up with a plan.

"He skirted their camp and headed north about four or five miles—set an old downed cottonwood afire. Threw a little bear grease from his possibles kit on fer good measure—makes nice, black smoke. He knew that smoke would get the curiosity of the war party. By the time he circled on back to the Kiowa camp, there was only two warriors holding the woman and child. Sam walks into camp, pretty as you please, with his buffler gun held 'bout chest high to one warrior, his rifle held on the other. One of 'em makes a move toward him and, well, he winds up with the spirits. The other stands there and watches as Sam takes his pony, seats the woman and child, jumps on his own hoss and takes off.

"He 'spected the Kiowa to follow and prob'ly have a shot at takin' his hair. Wasn't 'til years later he learned they turned his story into, well, a kinda parable, I guess. They wound up honorin' 'im fer bein' so clever."

Libby smiled at the story, thinking that it sounded like the hundred other Sam Tate tales she had heard over the years.

"Thank you for the story, Lieutenant," she said. "It does my heart good to hear of Sam's experiences. I feel he will bring Amos back to us. I feel it within my soul."

Keating nodded in agreement and resumed looking off south to the peaks. He cleared his throat and said, "Pardon me, ma'am, but ye must be near ready to fall on over from tiredness. Lemme walk ye on back to yore place so's ye can rest."

"Thank you, Mr. Keating," she said as they started across the clearing. As they neared the trading house, she saw Stephen move across the lit window, pacing the floor. She knew the remainder of the night would be long, indeed.

She thanked Keating again and stepped up on the boardwalk before turning around and speaking. "Mr. Keating, what became of the mother and child?"

Keating hesitated for a moment, then said, "Well, the mam was some sickly. She'd endured much on the prairie, and even more at the hands of the Kiowa. Sam said she lost a piece of her soul. Warn't two weeks later she went under in the shadow of the *Huajatolla*. She's buried up near Sam 'n Esther's place."

"How sad," Libby mused. "And the little girl?"

Keating hesitated, sighed, then continued with difficulty.

"She was a little dark-haired spitfire of a thing, awright." Keating let out another sharp sigh. "Esther had gave Sam a daughter two years before, little Mary. Then, when she saw that little orphan gal, Esther knew there'd be no separatin' them two childern. Esther 'n Sam kept her.

"Not too many know it, but that little girl became Sam's daughter, Miz Herold. Garcias kilt sweet Em'ly last week."

He paused for a moment, feeling Libby's shock.

"I'm sorry ma'am, but it's true. Em'ly Tate she was."

*"...he had fallen twice in the past hundred
yards, only to be dragged along..."*

CHAPTER EIGHT

THE PASS BETWEEN the Spanish Peaks and the Great Sand
Mountains had been traversed for centuries. Extending
west from the drainages of the Cucharas and Huerfano
Rivers, the land became a broad saddle leading up and
over the rim of the front range of the Rockies, down into
the broad, high desert valley formed by the Rio Grande
River, the San Luis Valley. The pass itself narrowed at the
top, becoming a gap that allowed travelers access to the
wide valleys and towering mountains of southwestern
Colorado.

The south side of the pass was heavily timbered with
varieties of spruce and fir, juniper, scrub oak, pinon pine
and vast groves of delicate, quaking aspen. The dense forest gave way to sage and pinon to the north, along with
fine grass in spring and fall. Several small streams gave the
pass excellent drainage, and various ravines and gulches
led to the high mountains located both north and south.
The dense southern forested slopes proved to be near-
impossible to traverse unless the various trails across the
pass were known.

The Utes had likely carved the first trails as they were
forced into the mountains by enemy tribes. The Mexicans
had used the pass for trade as far back as anyone

remembered. And many of the old Spanish families claimed that the *conquistadores,* and perhaps even Francisco Vásquez de Coronado himself, had passed through the area. Artifacts in the possession of many of these families served to verify such claims.

Because it was a natural highway through the nearly vertical mountains of the front range, La Veta Pass could be predicted as the route of first choice. Ordinarily, Sam Tate might have reasoned that the Garcias would follow another more obscure course, but with the death of Vivian and the wounding of Filipio, Tate speculated that the outlaws would be disjointed and lacking direction. By looping back through Herold's Crossing, they showed that they were headed home to roost, to disappear into the villages of New Mexico Territory. They had but two fairly direct routes, and La Veta Pass offered them the best shelter and the quickest passage to the Mexican villages south of the San Luis Valley.

Tate felt in his bones that they were headed over the pass. If he was wrong, it would likely be months before he could track them down, and Amos Herold would surely be killed at some point.

Tate was consumed by weariness. Perched on his saddle atop an unfamiliar horse, he looked back to the east at the barely lightening sky and shook his head to clear his wits. The past few days, he realized, had been the toughest of his life. Now, he had to push himself even harder.

He took off his battered felt hat, turned it upside down and poured water from his canteen into it. He quickly stuck the hat back on his head, soaking himself and allowing the water to trickle underneath his buckskins in the morning chill.

"Oughta keep this child from nappin'," he whispered through chattering teeth.

He had reached the eastern slope that led up into La Veta Pass, passing north of Huerfano Butte and Francisco's

Fort on the way. Although he could follow little sign in the darkness, the bright moonlight allowed him to navigate the countless ravines and arroyos that dotted the area. With the coming of the dawn, it was now time to head up the pass.

If his hunch about the Garcias' route turned out to be correct, he would have saved five or six hours by traveling at night, time that could prove crucial in catching the desperadoes.

"Well, Lancaster, ol' hoss," he said, "it's time to climb up the Saddle, make a sweep through the trees."

He lightly spurred the horse and held on as the magnificent animal effortlessly began following a trail into the trees. The horse cut across country at the rider's command, sweeping the area in the increasing light for signs of the outlaws and their hostage.

Tate ran across dozens of game trails cut through the forest, as well as two wider trails where ranchers had moved cattle up to ranches on the pass and down into the San Luis Valley.

As the sun rose higher, he took to the ground, and carefully led the horse through wide clearings of underbrush and saplings. Moving to the south, he neared the upslope of the pass, where the steep grade forced travelers to stay below. He passed through the area several times before noticing a tiny pine bent to the ground near a lichen-covered boulder. He carefully made his way toward the small tree and, as he neared, saw the tracks of two horses, the same horses he'd followed from the arroyo near the Arkansas River. With growing excitement, he allowed himself to finally believe that he'd been right.

His eye caught a slight depression in some moss and soft dirt a foot away, and he slowly studied it. As his eyes became accustomed to the trail, he noticed the same depressions every two or three feet.

Footprints. He studied them more carefully, following

them for several yards, and finally discerned a sharp edge that crushed into the ground—a heel. So, no moccasined Indian was following the outlaws on foot, as he had originally thought. They had put Amos Herold aground and were forcing him to walk.

He returned to the stallion, which was eagerly grazing on long, sweet grass.

"Them divils is on up ahead, Lancaster 'ol lad," he whispered to the horse. Smiling, he reached in a saddlebag to pull out a piece of dried beef. He bit off the end and laughed to himself as he began to chew.

"Yep, hoss, ol' Beelzebub hisself's gonna pay 'em a visit."

Amos Herold was very close to wishing he were dead.

His legs felt as if they would no longer work, and he had fallen twice in the past hundred yards, only to be dragged along by the rope binding him to Filipio Garcia's saddle horn. The solidly wound lasso was looped twice around his midsection before tightly binding his hands and leading to the saddle. It was only twelve feet long, forcing the boy to walk quickly behind the outlaw's horse.

He had been walking since the outlaws reached the foot of La Veta Pass, and he was exhausted. His petrifying fear had been overcome by fatigue as he forced one foot in front of the other up the mountain pass. He had a long gash above one eye that kept opening, letting blood seep down and blind him. He had to trot faster than the walking horse in order to lift his sleeve to the wound to wipe it.

Although the previous day and night were a blur, he forced himself to think back on what had happened in order to keep his wits about him. He had been playing with the rope of the bucket leading down to the well water when he heard shots toward the corral. By the time he realized something was going on, he was slammed from behind and thrown to the ground. It was only when he tried to roll over that he realized he had been attacked by one of the Garcias. He immediately panicked, thinking it was the man he shot who had come back to kill him. But deep inside, through the panic, he was his parents' child, and when pushed, his first instinct was to push back. A mad streak began to run through him.

As Filipio Garcia dragged him up from the ground, he began to fight the outlaw, kicking and biting. It was then that Garcia slashed the gun across his forehead, stunning him momentarily. He remembered being lugged to the thicket and tossed to the ground before Garcia shot at some unknown target. Then, he was being dragged through the thicket. Once, he broke away and almost escaped when Garcia tripped, but his captor reached him just as he was nearing a clearing and whipped a rawhide cord around his wrists, binding them together. He was roughly hauled upright and felt Garcia's forearm around his throat. He heard the man's heavy breathing.

In a thick accent, he said, "No more! I will shoot you down! Do you understand?"

Amos had nodded as the outlaw led him into the clearing. But try as he might, he couldn't be docile for long. He began struggling again. The next thing he knew, he heard Garcia scream and was thrown to the ground. He rolled and sat up, then saw a knife sticking from the back of the outlaw's left arm. The shock of the sight rendered him momentarily frozen, and he missed his best chance to slip off into the thicket. Instead, he stayed put on the ground and listened as bullets whipped over the outlaw's head and back into the thicket.

Cursing and obviously in great pain, Filipio Garcia reached down for the boy, grabbed his arm, and ran to the outlaw's horse. Repeating his threats, he forced Amos onto his mount and was immediately on behind him, a small yelp of pain escaping his lips. Garcia spurred the horse and they were off at a gallop.

Riding in front of the pommel near the horse's neck with his bound hands entwined in its mane, Amos looked to his right and saw his father lying on the ground, rolling toward the thicket. Vivian Garcia, the one Amos had shot, was pointing a gun at his father. Amos screamed in denial at the same time he heard a huge roar and saw what looked like a gallon of red paint explode from the outlaw's back. Someone had shot him!

Then they were beyond the thicket and adjacent clump of trees, and he was flying across the plains, a prisoner. He tried to look back but was cuffed on the neck by the outlaw's chin. Garcia yelled, "No!" at him, and he looked ahead, holding on for dear life at the same time.

They rode for nearly 15 minutes at a full-out gallop before pulling up on the top of a lightly-wooded hill from which the prairie spread out to the east. To the west, a series of broad flood plains fanned out toward the foothills, a rugged, hilly and pinon covered expanse offering excellent protection from anyone following. The place had obviously been chosen beforehand for its command of the area as an ideal starting point for evading pursuit.

Garcia halted the nearly-exhausted horse in a slight depression at the top of the hill and, with his right arm, threw Amos to the ground. The boy hit hard on his side and rolled on his back, lying still for a moment to assess any damage. When he realized he had only been shaken up and not really hurt, he sat up in time to see Filipio Garcia slowly slide off the right side of the horse. The sweat dripped from under the outlaw's dusty hat, down the back of his longish hair onto his collar and fairly soaked the back of his rough shirt. The knife handle stuck awkwardly from the back of Garcia's arm as he sidled toward Amos.

"Get up and move over there," he said, indicating some scrub oak and sagebrush a few yards away. Through his fear and anger, Amos detected the outlaw's pain, and was amazed Garcia had the strength to carry on with the blade buried in his arm.

Garcia motioned for Amos to stand still while he looked around the area. Finally, he looked back toward the boy, his face drained of color and his breath coming quickly.

"I want you to listen to me very carefully, young Herold. My brother Vivian is obviously very, very dead," he chuckled before he continued, "and Santiago is God knows where. It looks like you're going to have to pull this knife out of me."

Amos instinctively shook his head back and forth out of sheer amazement. The outlaw had kidnapped him, and now told him to remove a knife. It was absurd.

Seeing the doubt and incredulity in Amos's stare, Garcia quickly backhanded him across the face with his right hand. Amos recoiled from the sting and reached up with his bound hands to wipe the tears from his eyes as the outlaw palmed his revolver from its holster at lightning speed and aimed it at the boy. It seemed as if the action had hurt Garcia more than it had Amos, as Filipio inhaled in pain and held his breath. After a few tense moments, he lowered the gun and aimed it toward the ground. Taking yet another deep breath, he continued.

"Here's how it will be done. You'll gently grab the knife handle, and when I nod, you'll hold it still while I pull away. Do you understand?"

Amos nodded without speaking.

"Good. You are a smart young man, I think. Smart enough to know that if you did anything to hurt me, or if you tried to run, I would shoot you dead on the spot. You know that, don't you?" Amos swallowed out of sheer fear and nodded to the affirmative.

Garcia then pushed the boy back toward a tree and ordered him to stand with his back against it. With one hand, the desperado looped a rope around both tree and boy, leaving Amos's bound hands free and tightening the

115

coil until he could hardly breathe.

"Now," said Garcia, "now, I will back up to you. You will grab the handle firmly. If you twist it or turn it or cause me any pain at all, I'll shoot you and leave you to die here against this tree."

Holding the pistol in his right hand, Garcia turned around and backed up to the boy.

"Now, grab it!" he commanded.

Amos lifted his hands and awkwardly positioned them to where he could grasp the handle by inverting his right hand. The weakness in his bound arms was appreciable, and it was all he could do to stop his hands from shaking as he grabbed the dark, weighted wood handle. He noticed that no blade showed, the knife had gone in to the hilt, with only the four-inch handle protruding from the blood-soaked shirt sleeve.

"Hold it tight!" growled Garcia. He took a deep breath and thrust himself forward. As he did so, he stifled a scream and fell to the ground, writhing in pain. He lay there momentarily, then rose to his knees and looked up at the boy. The vehemence in the desperado's face was frightening. Then, still on his knees, Garcia lowered his head to the ground, gasping for air, and was motionless.

Amos was surprised at how easily the knife slipped out, and he now held it in front of him. The blade was streaked with blood, and he thought he might vomit if any was wiped on him. He stared at the knife dumbly, not knowing what to do with it. Finally, he dropped it to the ground and began wrestling with the rope that held him. As he struggled, he thought about the outlaw's wound. His father had taught him how to handle any variety of injury, so he had a general idea of the seriousness of Garcia's wound. Obviously, it had not been imbedded in bone. So the only real danger would be the possibility of excessive bleeding. Perhaps Garcia was bleeding to death.

He managed to loosen the rope enough to breathe

comfortably and was thinking ahead, figuring out how to grab the prostrate outlaw's pistol, when a horse and rider leaped through the sage and came to an awkward halt before him. His heart sank as Santiago Garcia jumped from the saddle, looked quickly around, and slipped a rifle from its scabbard. He walked up to Amos, wariness in his eyes. "Is he dead?" the young outlaw asked in an accent even thicker than his uncle's. He was staring at Filipio's motionless form.

Amos shook his head back and forth to indicate that he didn't know. The young *pistolero* gently nudged his uncle with his boot. Filipio Garcia let out a savage groan and twisted his head into the ground, all the while holding his wounded arm with his right hand. Slowly, he sat upright, his dark face red from the blood that had run to his cheeks in his upside down position. He shook his head to clear it and attempted to stand. His dizziness caused him to sit down flat on his rear, crushing the hat that had earlier fallen from his head. After a few moments, he turned over on his side and retched, all the while being watched by the two boys.

Presently, Filipio held his good hand out to Santiago, who pulled him to his feet. After a few unsteady steps, Garcia asked for water. After he had swallowed nearly a canteen full, he poured the rest over his head and let it run down through his matted hair. He then had Santiago help him remove his shirt to assess the wound.

Pulling a rag from his saddlebag, Santiago poured water on it and cleaned the wound as well as he could, then laid the soaked rag against the wound and bound it in place with a strip from another rag. After making sure the wound was bound tightly, he helped Filipio put the bloody shirt back on.

Filipio once more shook his head to clear it, then looked around and took in the area. He looked back toward Santiago, cleared his throat and spit on the ground.

"So where were you, nephew?" he asked sarcastically in Spanish. His eyes bored into Santiago, forcing the young outlaw to stare at the ground.

"I, I, thought we were under attack, Filipio. I, um, shot at one of the men and thought, I thought..."

"You thought nothing, you cowardly pig!" shouted Filipio. "You ran like a dog."

Santiago shook his head in denial, never lifting his gaze.

"Did you watch Vivian die, coward?" taunted Filipio.

The comment was like a slap in Santiago's face.

"Vivian is dead?" he asked dumbly.

"Yes, nephew, yes. By the look of it, there will be little left to bury. I believe from the sound it was likely a buffalo gun that sent your uncle to dwell with his precious Virgin.

"At least now he can drive her loco, and leave me in peace," he muttered.

Garcia looked his nephew up and down and finally shook his head in disgust. Then, thinking clearly, he said, "Keep a lookout. They should be following shortly. I want them to think they have us at a disadvantage. Then we'll slip away and travel through the night for distance.

"We go north of the *Huajatolla,* over the Saddle Pass and finally down to San Luis."

Santiago was suddenly tired of being upbraided, tired of taking orders. He gathered his courage and his practiced sneer, and blurted out his accusation.

"Why are we here anyway, Uncle? You couldn't stand up to a loco *woman* like Vivian? If we had gone north, nothing would have happened."

Filipio gave his nephew a withering stare before busting out laughing. He held his wounded arm tighter as he broke into peals of laughter. Finally, he brought himself under control and wiped his eyes with his forearm.

"Oh, Santiago. You are truly an idiot," he said, still chuckling. "Do you think we go anywhere for a *reason?* The only *reason* we have for doing anything is to be chased, to feel the fear of a dog on the run. You haven't figured that out yet, my young *pistolero?*"

Filipio began laughing again while Santiago looked on, his braggadocio's rashness now tamed and his eyes wide in both wonder and fear.

"Vivian was...Vivian," continued Filipio. "I had no reason to go anywhere else, or with anyone else. We did fine for many years, did we not? We took what we wanted, killed when we wanted, and followed Vivian's dreams. It made him happy.

"The plan to return to Herold's was a good one, an interesting one," he said matter-of-factly. "If you had not started shooting out of panic, we likely would have dined tonight on freshly killed beef while I entertained Herold's woman."

Filipio looked wistfully back across the stretch of land and sighed heavily. He limped slowly past Santiago, stopped and turned, and hit the young outlaw full in the face with a mighty backhand.

As Santiago crumpled to the ground, his rifle flying from his hand, Filipio grabbed his wounded arm and grimaced. Still, he managed to smile.

"Now, Santiago, get up from the dirt and watch for those who follow us. If you want to live to whimper and run another day, you'd best have sharp eyes."

Santiago stood and held his hand across his bleeding nose. The blood dripped from between his fingers as he picked up his rifle and made for a small rise, plopping down on his stomach to oversee the landscape spread out before him. Filipio did the same, easing himself down behind a boulder and sighting a rifle out over the red and brown vista.

Amos Herold watched the exchange with fascination, nearly forgetting the fear gnawing at his stomach. Although he spoke serviceable Spanish, he picked up little from the incident, just enough to know that the two outlaws were at odds. As his father had taught him, once divided, something can never be put back together. He mulled over the situation and decided to look for ways in which he could further distance the outlaws from each other.

It had been less than an hour before Amos saw Filipio pick up a stone and throw it in Santiago's direction. He pointed to the northeast, and began to fire. Santiago did the same, firing a round every ten seconds or so. For several minutes, the outlaws kept up the regular fire, while now and again, a far-off shot boomed in return.

The sun was slowly slipping behind the mountains as the exchange continued, and Amos's initial elation at his possible rescue began to pale. He had heard Filipio's plan to slip out in the darkness, and realized what was happening. The outlaws had someone pinned down and unable to approach. When darkness came, they would slip out, either taking him with them or killing him on the spot.

He kept working on the ropes, but this time with new intensity. He was close to slipping the loop down around his hips when he looked up and saw Filipio Garcia staring back at him. The outlaw slowly turned his rifle around and pointed it at the boy. Fighting the urge to close his eyes and whimper, Amos summoned all of his courage and stared directly down the rifle's barrel. Lifting his eyes, he stared deep into those of the outlaw. He was reminded of those times he had stared directly into the eyes of one of the dogs the Herolds kept as pets. The same incessant hunger and impatience flashed back from the outlaw's eyes. There was no connection, no understanding. Merely a contest to see whose soul could stand up to raw scrutiny.

The boy instinctively knew that Garcia would break first, either by firing the rifle and ending Amos's life, or by averting his gaze. When the outlaw quickly looked away, lowered the rifle and began crawling toward Amos, he felt an odd sense of accomplishment. He knew he'd won a battle, and that he had the ammunition to somehow beat this hard, ruthless man.

Garcia made his way to the boy and slowly stood next to him. Looking uneasily at Amos, he tucked the rifle under his good arm and with the same hand, reached out and grabbed the rope.

"Now, young Herold, we will begin a chase," he said. "I suspect the men shooting up here are the ones who shot Vivian in two. Perhaps one is even the Spirit, Sam Tate. Am I right?"

Amos made no answer, but suddenly thought for the first time about the shooting of Vivian Garcia. His father was on the ground, and neither of his brothers had access to a gun powerful enough to blow clear through Garcia's body. And who had thrown the knife that imbedded itself in Filipio's arm? Perhaps Sam Tate had arrived, or maybe the soldiers Tate mentioned when he met with Amos's father on his way to track the killers along the Cucharas River. In any event, there were more men in pursuit then merely his brothers.

Filipio continued to stare at Amos, both his curiosity and his need to speak evident. Finally, he said, "This was not necessary, you know. I did not know about the Gorner woman, who she was. If I had known she was Tate's daughter, maybe we would have just passed on by. Who knows? But now that Tate comes, I must disappear with my people."

He chuckled lightly and continued sarcastically. "*My* people, I call them. One of them is as likely to shoot me from behind as any of you *gringos*. It is hard, young Herold, to have no place to go."

His tone abruptly changed to one of business.

"Now, you will speak, or I will kill you. Was Tate at your home today?"

Amos hesitated, then realized that the truth was as good as a lie. He had to answer and hope that the outlaw believed him.

121

"No, Sam wasn't there," he said. "Nobody was there, just my Dad and Mama and brothers. Nobody else."

"Ah, then, who do you suppose sank a knife into my arm?" asked the outlaw menacingly.

"I don't know. I truly don't."

A bullet spat on the ground ten yards away, causing Filipio to crouch and spin around. He quickly turned back, looked at Amos, and continued.

"It doesn't matter, I suppose. Now listen closely. I think you may be of value. If I keep you as a hostage, I can bargain. So, here is what you will do.

"We will now walk to Santiago's horse and you will mount in front on the saddle, as before. If you run or try to spur the horse, you die."

Garcia painfully unlooped the rope binding Amos, then roughly shoved the boy toward Santiago's horse. Behind them, the young outlaw continued to shoot intermittently toward his target.

Once Amos was mounted, Garcia tied his feet together tightly beneath the horse, just behind its front legs. Then, he loosened the boy's hands and tied them together around the horses neck, forcing the boy to lay flat against the animal. The horse attempted to rear twice, trying to readjust the odd weight on its shoulders and neck. Finally, it calmed down as Garcia looped its reins around a high branch.

Filipio gave a short, high whistle, calling Santiago. The young desperado came at a trot, quickly sheathing his rifle and jumping on the horse. Filipio, with great effort, hauled himself into his saddle.

They set out into the twilight, carefully picking their way across the broad landscape and through the foothills. Occasionally, they would hear a rifle report behind them, rightly figuring that the pursuers were testing their position, figuring how and when to approach.

In the awkward position, thrown across the horse's

neck, Amos could scarcely breathe. His ribs were jolted in rhythm with the horse's gait, and he could only attempt to cushion the shock by leaning to one side or the other. Yet each time he did so, the horse began throwing its head, and Santiago would punch him in the kidneys.

The torture went on for miles, until the group was traveling in total darkness, in the shadow of the front range. When he thought he could take no more, the horses suddenly pulled up. Santiago jumped to the ground and conferred with Filipio, who was but a ghost in the darkness that covered the steep mountains.

Amos lifted his head and looked back to the east, seeing that the vast plain was eerily moonlit. The moon had yet to rise high enough above the westerly mountains to light the outlaws' way, yet they seemed intent on forging their way up the pass.

After a short conference, Santiago began untying Amos's legs and hands. Once accomplished, he pushed the boy over the side of the horse. Amos's entire body seemed to be numb, and he found that he could not stand at the same time that crippling needles began piercing his limbs. It was all he could do to keep from crying out as the pain signaled the return of blood to his limbs.

While Amos lay on the ground, Santiago fashioned a lasso from a long rope, testing it against his saddle pommel. When he was satisfied, he tied the rope to the elder desperado's saddle horn. He kicked Amos twice to force him to stand. After the second kick, Amos jumped to his feet and stood fiercely in Santiago's face. The shocked outlaw stepped back and swallowed hard, not knowing what to do. Amos was about to go for his throat when the silence was broken by the cocking of a pistol. Both young men looked toward Filipio, whose shadowlike form was broken only by the reflection of his smile in the moonlight.

"Do not make me shoot you, young Herold," the outlaw

said in a cheerful voice. "I may have need of you, and I'd rather not take the time to hide your body right now."

Amos stifled his urge to either fight or bolt, and stood staring at Filipio with murder in his eyes. Presently, Santiago stepped behind Amos and secured the makeshift rigging. Still sore, the boy could not imagine that the outlaws would literally drag him up La Veta Pass, but as Filipio's horse took off in a brisk walk, he knew it to be true.

Now, hours later and nearing first light, Amos felt he could walk no further. The rough landscape had sapped his strength, and he thought that if he should fall, he would not rise again.

He walked numbly along, stumbling occasionally and taking scant notice that dawn was about to break. His thirst was enormous, yet it still took minutes for him to notice that a new sound had broken the monotony. The rush of a small creek could be heard. The splashing sound of the water was like a siren's call to his ears, beckoning him, telling him that a price would be paid for a cool, sweet drink.

Then, the horses halted. He inadvertently sat, knowing that when they took off again, he would be dragged. But he was beyond caring.

He heard the two outlaws conferring and caught a few phrases. And then it hit him. The smell. Bacon was frying somewhere! The odor caused his stomach to churn, and he realized his thirst was rivaled by his hunger.

Both outlaws dismounted and Filipio walked back toward the boy while Santiago removed the loop connected to Amos from his uncle's saddle horn.

Filipio looked at Amos, chuckled, then spoke.

"Well, young Herold. You have had quite a walk. Now you will rest while we find some breakfast. I believe the miner below will prove to be a useful host.

"Now, Santiago will tie you to a tree. You will make no

sound, of course. If you do, you die. It is simple."

Amos managed to croak, then hoarsely speak.

"Water. I need water."

"When we return, you'll have water. First, we must visit the men below."

Now Amos understood the plan. Down the narrow canyon, someone was working a placer claim. There must be more than one, for Filipio had mentioned "men." The outlaws would kill them, then steal their belongings before continuing.

The nightmare was growing worse and worse.

Santiago grabbed Amos under the arms from behind and threw the rope over a high branch of a lightning-struck pine. He then pulled the rope until Amos was elevated on his tiptoes. The young outlaw then tied the rope to a lower branch, leaving Amos virtually swinging in the air.

"Yes, nephew, I believe that will do," said Filipio. "Only one more thing."

The outlaw approached Amos with his knife and menacingly held it to the boy's throat. He began chuckling and then swiftly cut the boy's sleeve, grabbed the gaping hole and pulled downward. He wadded the cloth up and forced it into Amos's mouth before the startled boy could protest. From behind, Santiago drew another filthy strip of cloth around Amos's mouth, tying it behind his head.

"Now, young Herold," said Filipio, "you will not feel the need to warn anyone that they are about to have visitors.

"You will be quiet and not move until we return."

The outlaw gently patted Amos's face as the boy returned his stare with a glare. He slapped the boy with his right hand, spat on the ground, and walked away.

Amos was surprised when the two outlaws mounted their horses rather than leaving them. He figured the miner's camp must be further than he thought. But then it occurred to him that they were attempting to act the part of weary travelers stumbling on a friendly camp.

The boy looked up at his hands and began to work them in the rope. They were tightly bound, the rope being knotted from the pressure of pulling the boy up the steep side of the pass.

Seeing that there was little he could do to loosen his hands, he began studying his surroundings. Despite his weariness, he felt he might be able to swing himself by the rope over the the low branch where the rope's end was knotted. If he could pull himself up over the taut rope, the knot might slip, or the branch might break, slackening the rope and letting him escape.

The tips of his boots were barely touching the ground as he pushed himself forward. He started swinging, then tensed his body and surged forward in rhythm to increase the swinging motion. He began spinning around while swinging and fought to keep his back and forth motion. Finally, after two attempts, he swung a leg up over the length of rope leading from the tree. He was stuck in midair, and moaned in despair. He kept working his other leg until it, too, was up over the rope. He locked his legs and began swinging back and forth, frantically watching the small branch to which the rope was knotted.

He had little time to celebrate as he watched the knot begin to slip, stripping pine needles as it fairly ripped down the length of the branch. Amos fell hard to the ground, landing on his side, and was immediately up. He pulled on the rope and began working at his hands. In a few minutes, he had loosened the knot enough to slip his left hand out. Shaking the rope off, he furiously ripped the strip of cloth from his face and spat out the wad of shirt-sleeve in his mouth.

He stood and stretched, shaking his limbs to regain circulation. Realizing there was little time, he fled swiftly down the trail the outlaws had followed. After a third-mile or so, he was at the edge of a steep ravine cut by the fierce mountain stream below. As he rounded a corner, he saw fifty yards ahead, two men huddled near a campfire, one sitting and one standing. A rifle was across the lap of the sitting man, while the man standing was unarmed. The Garcias were on horseback, talking to the men. Then, the standing man motioned for the outlaws to dismount and join them.

Without thinking, Amos screamed with all his might.

"No! They'll kill you! They're the Garcias! No! Arm yourselves!"

Amos watched as the four faces turned toward him. He continued screaming.

"No! Listen to me! They'll kill you! *They'll kill you!*"

The boy watched as Filipio Garcia smoothly pulled his rifle from its scabbard and swung it around in his direction. He nearly felt the rifle spit and instinctively jumped to his left.

As his feet went out from under him, he saw the bullet hit a tree where he had been standing. Then, he was over the edge of the ravine, screaming as he crashed down the steep, boulder-strewn embankment toward the roiling water.

*"...it was a privilege to mine gold from
streams under God's blue sky..."*

CHAPTER NINE

NARVEL SPRIGGS WAS a hard rock miner from Kentucky
who had heard much about Colorado's Pikes Peak area. So
much, in fact, that he walked into town one day in 1860,
sold all of his possessions except his squirrel gun, saddled
up his mule, and made his way alone across the great
American desert. No one had to tell him what a foolish
thing he was doing. He knew that strength lay in numbers,
and that his number was one. He reckoned that his hair
would likely hang in a Comanche lodge, but his life was
more than mundane, it was practically nonexistent. He figured any adventure was worth the price.

He reached the twin settlements of Auraria and Denver
at the confluence of the South Platte River and Cherry
Creek, in the shadow of the mighty Rocky Mountains, with
little more than a thirst for good Kentucky sour mash. He
knew that he'd done the right thing. Spriggs immediately
headed up Russell Gulch, where he fell in with a group
of southern miners led by the other flamboyant
Georgian, Green Russell, and his partner, Decatur "Kate"
Patterson. The group had founded Auraria, naming it after
their home town in Georgia, before they moved on up
into the mountains.

In those first few months, Spriggs solidified a strong

friendship with Wylie Morris, one of the Georgia party. When Russell and Patterson decided to make a run back to Georgia in order to demonstrate their support for the Confederate States of America, Spriggs wanted no part of the expedition. He convinced Morris that the two of them would be better off mining in the Rockies. Morris agreed, and the two men began roaming the mountains in a seemingly never-ending search for gold.

Although a hard rock miner by trade, Spriggs took to placer mining, and in no time seemed as good at it as anyone in the territory. Morris questioned him, and was told that all in all, it was a privilege to mine gold from streams under God's blue sky, while it was a job to haul ore from the darkness hundreds of feet down into the devil's territory. Morris shook his head and supposed that was so.

The two set up small placers throughout the central front range of the Rockies, every once in a while having a brush with Indians or claim jumpers, but generally faring very well, indeed. By 1865, with thousands of miners continuing to flood the Denver area, they decided to move their operations down to the southern mountains, where they'd heard reports of accessible water and fine mineral deposits. They understood that Patterson and Russell had failed in their attempt to return to Georgia, and were sitting out the war near John Francisco's Fort. They stopped in and spent a few days at Kate Patterson's spread near Huerfano Butte, before heading off over La Veta pass on their way to the Sangre de Cristos. That had been three months ago, before they found a nice, accessible vein of ore that looked like it might play out well near the eastern summit of La Veta Pass.

Spriggs was surprised to see two men hail his camp so early in the morning. It was sometimes hard to hear over the ever present rush of the stream, and he was edgy about the possibility of running into Utes. Consequently, his Kentucky squirrel rifle never left his possession. He had just donned his thick denim pants, drawn his suspenders over his wool shirt, and slapped his hat on his head. He was busy stirring bacon around the cast iron frying pan when he saw movement down the access trail to their camp. He slowly slid the rifle over his lap and continued stirring, acting as if he were unaware of the two shabby riders heading into camp.

He let out a quick whistle, a prearranged signal, to Morris, who emerged from a lean-to that served as shelter, while straightening his short brimmed hat and ambling over to the campfire.

"Comp'ny," said Spriggs in a soft Dixie drawl. "Don't look too sprightly, either. Check 'em out as they come in."

As the riders approached, Spriggs noticed their disheveled look. One seemed to be only a boy, his features hidden under a black hat that was almost large enough to be a sombrero. The other was hatless and seemed to favor his left side, holding his arm motionless, crossed in front of him. Spriggs could tell they were likely up to no good and told Morris to keep a watchful eye. But Morris was as impetuous as Spriggs was wary. True to his good nature, he left his pistol hanging on a saddle draped over a felled log.

The older rider stopped and waved his right hand to the two miners, silently requesting permission to approach the camp. Morris waved them in as Spriggs continued to scrutinize the pair. Both had sheathed rifles attached to their saddles and pistols in well-oiled holsters hanging at their sides. Obviously Mexican, the older rider was sporting several days' growth of beard, and as he approached, dark stains were visible on his ragged shirt, particularly on the sleeve of the left arm—blood!

The horses picked their way over to the campsite, stopping several yards from the miners. The horses were lathered, and had obviously traveled some distance, through the night no less. Spriggs began to feel even more edgy about the visitors. It didn't hurt to be cautious, he told himself.

Spriggs continued to sit, his rifle plainly across his lap, while Morris took a step toward the riders.

"Hep you, boys?" he said. "Looks like you might need it."

Filipio Garcia looked down at the man, judged him, and slowly favored him with a broad smile.

"Gracias, señor," he said. Switching to English, he continued. "We have come far and were set upon by bandits— roadmen— as we started up this pass."

Morris shook his head in understanding while Spriggs wondered to himself who would be foolish enough to set upon a well-armed duo like this. Spriggs spoke up.

"Someone tried to bushwhack you? Well, how many was there?"

"Three," answered Filipio. "I believe my nephew here and I managed to wound at least two of them, but as you can see, one of them hit me in the arm."

"From behind, I see," said Spriggs. "Musta been behind you."

"Yes, they must have been," said Garcia warily.

"Hmm," said Spriggs, letting the accusation hang in the air. "S'pose they followed you up the pass?"

"I think not. As I said, we shot them," said Garcia, now irritable.

"Well," Morris broke in. "if'n you need some aid, we'll hep you. Got some medicine in a pack around here someplace. We'll throw a little more fatback on the fire, git you boys fat 'n happy."

"Once again, *gracias,"* said Garcia.

Morris motioned for the riders to dismount and join them. Santiago was halfway off his horse when the yelling started. Surprised, the four men looked at each other before figuring out where the ruckus was coming from.

There, in a break in the trees overlooking the canyon, stood a boy, hatless with his shirt ripped. He jumped up and down in an agitated manner, and his hands were cupped around his mouth. He was frantically yelling something. The rush of the stream made his words largely unintelligible, but Spriggs managed to make out some of the language, his face screwed up in an expression of confusion as he repeated it to himself.

"Garcias? No? Kill...*They'll kill you!*"

Suddenly, the older of the two riders, who had yet to dismount, whipped his rifle from its scabbard and, in one smooth motion, aimed at the boy and pulled the trigger. The boy immediately jumped to his left, disappearing over the edge of the steep ravine that led down to the river.

At the same time, Spriggs stood, the shock wearing off as he raised his rifle. Seeing the miner rise in the corner of his eye, Filipio Garcia immediately spurred his horse forward through the campfire, knocking Spriggs to the ground. As Garcia fought to control the animal and bring it about, Morris made a break for his pistol. Turned halfway around, Garcia painfully ejected the spent shell from his rifle and, fairly growling in pain and frustration, fired off a shot at the running miner, hitting him in midstride. Morris rolled several times, coming to a halt with his right arm bent at an impossible angle below him and a bright streak of crimson where his throat had been.

Santiago Garcia had remounted his horse and was attempting to turn toward the trees when Spriggs came up from the ground, raised his rifle, and shot at the boy's head. Simultaneously, the young outlaw's horse stepped in a depression in the ground, nearly going down. The stumble caused the shot to miss, grazing Santiago on the neck and continuing upward, putting a finger-sized hole through his hat. Seeing that the boy was running scared and sensing the position of the older outlaw, Spriggs quickly turned and ran to his right toward the stream, only to see Filipio Garcia leveling the rifle at him. Garcia had him dead to rights. All he could do was lunge for the cover of a group of willows growing near the water. Steeling

133

himself for a shot that did not come, Spriggs scampered deeper into the foliage, only to see Garcia frantically working the lever action of the rifle.

The outlaw cursed loudly and raked his spurs across his exhausted horse's withers. The horse reared, then took off like a lightning bolt. The outlaw was into the trees before Spriggs could get off a shot.

Running to his right, Spriggs saw the rear of the young outlaw's horse disappear around a stand of aspen. He continued to run up a steep embankment, hoping to be able to cut the outlaws off at the trail.

He was panting from both exertion and fear as he crested the top of the hill, only to see the two mounted outlaws rounding a curve some 40 yards ahead. He raised his rifle and quickly lowered it in frustration. They were gone, and knowing the ways of desperate men on the frontier, he felt they would not be back. There were other camps to raid, other miners to kill.

Garcias! How stupid of him not to suspect. Word was that there were three of them, though. He was uneasy, wondering if the retreat was a ruse, with the third outlaw hanging back, ready to attack. He pushed the thought into the back of his mind, rationalizing that the two outlaws he had seen likely were too destitute and tired to cook up such a plan. Still, he resolved to exercise extreme caution.

He made his way back down the hill as quickly as possible. He knew that Morris's wound was fatal, but he had to look him over anyway.

He approached his partner with dread, and dutifully checked for any signs of life. He finally made himself directly examine the grievous wound in Morris's neck, and reckoned that his friend was killed instantly by what he calculated as a shot that relied more on blind luck than ability. He picked Morris up, smearing blood down his shirt, and carried the broken, lifeless body into the shade of the lean-to.

"Aw, Wylie. Dammit," he said to the friend he carried in his arms. "You always did trust folks too much. Now look what's gone and happened."

He gently laid the body down and covered it with a thick wool blanket to discourage the vermin and varmints until a proper grave could be dug. He said a short prayer, then turned to the task at hand.

He saw the boy who had shouted a warning go over the ravine's edge like a young crow on its first flight. Now, in thanks for the warning, he had to go find the boy's body. He had to see if there was any identification on him that could lead to some kin. And he had to bury him here beside Wylie.

He walked the 50 or so yards to the spot where the boy had been standing. He noticed the fresh bullet scar on the tree, its light wood splintered out from under the dark bark. He edged over to the brink of the ravine and looked down, trying to locate the boy's body. He could see nothing.

Nearly falling himself, he began descending the steep slope, following the disturbed ground where the boy's rolling body had created a crude path through the rocks and brush. He supposed the body had entered the water and was swept downstream. Indeed, the rapid water resulting from the high country's snowmelt resembled nothing more than a furious maelstrom making its way down the mountain canyon.

Spriggs began the arduous walk down the canyon, hoping that the boy's body had hung up on a branch or rock outcropping where he could retrieve it. He stopped briefly to take a few breaths and shake off the shock of attack. He gladly noted that the forest's wildlife was undisturbed, indicating no other men were in the area. As he watched, a fat doe disappeared between two trees across the stream, her muley ears and white tail bobbing through the thick brush and willows. Two curious bluejays cruised

135

overhead, flitting from spruce to spruce, their jabbering veiled by the roar of the water.

As Spriggs continued hiking, he noticed one of the jays diving toward the ground up ahead, landing and strutting toward something, a dead fish or mouse, no doubt. As he rounded the river's curve, he saw the bird examining something. As it came into view, he saw that it was a hand, the boy's hand! He rushed to the spot and saw the boy lying face up, his head on the rocky bank and his body in a pool of icy water near the stream's edge. He had been carried down the river, and apparently floated out of the eddy as the current negotiated a sharp turn, creating the pool to its opposite side.

Spriggs plunged into the freezing water and grabbed the boy, hurling him out of the stream and onto the pine needles covering the plush bank. The curious jay panicked and flew to a nearby spruce where it sat and watched the man put his ear to the boy's chest. As Spriggs suspected, he wasn't breathing. He quickly turned the prostrate boy on his stomach and began smacking him between the shoulder blades, trying to dislodge water and perhaps shock his heart. Then he turned him over and pushed hard on the chest, forcing up water from the lungs. The boy let loose a couple of tiny coughs, then was struggling to inhale. Spriggs sat him up so that he could gulp down great lungsfull of air. The boy then rolled over on his side, vomited for what seemed like minutes, then passed out cold.

Taking care to monitor the boy's breathing, Spriggs picked the boy up and began the arduous task of carrying him back up to camp. He weighed upwards of 120 pounds, Spriggs figured, and was stout to boot.

Spriggs struggled up the long hill, finally setting the boy to rest under a low-branched pine. Wiping the sweat from his forehead, he retrieved a medical kit from his saddlebag and began to attend to what seemed like dozens of wounds and scrapes inflicted by the fall. The rushing water had done an adequate job of washing the boy's blood away, and to Spriggs' surprise there seemed to be only one injury of note, a ring finger on the left hand that was bent at a 90 degree angle straight backward. Taking advantage of the boy's unconsciousness, Spriggs grabbed the broken finger and set it as best he could, then bound it tightly between two pieces of bark and wrapped it with a rawhide strip.

Having done all he could, Spriggs grabbed his rifle and took off to scout the area around the camp, making sure that the assailants had indeed left the area. Finding no sign after an hour's search, he returned, grabbed a pick and shovel, and sought a suitable spot for Morris's grave. He chose a site beneath the branches of a broad spruce and began digging. The ground was soft from recent rain and snowmelt, so the chore went quickly. By midafternoon, he was ready to inter his friend. First, he checked on the boy and, finding him warm, decided to move him into the lean-to. This required him to prepare Morris's body for burial quickly and to move it to the gravesite. Spriggs entered the lean-to and steeled himself for dealing with the body of his companion. First, he emptied the pockets and gathered the man's meager possessions. He intended on dividing up their diggings and sending Morris's share along with his belongings back to his family in Georgia. He quickly went through his friend's things, finding a small leather purse tucked into a saddlebag. In it were a few bills, a deed for five acres in Union County, Georgia, and a tintype photograph of a young woman, a girl really. Morris had never made mention of the girl, and Spriggs was left to wonder at his companion's secrets.

Spriggs lifted Morris's body onto the wool blanket and wrapped it tightly. Gently, he dragged the body out of the lean-to, across the camp clearing, and to the edge of the fresh grave.

Leaving the body, he returned to Amos and picked him up from his resting place. The boy stirred, opened his eyes and stared at Spriggs. He gave the miner a quizzical look, then passed once more into unconsciousness.

Spriggs carried Amos to the lean-to and gently placed him on the ground. A cool breeze blew through the open western side of the structure, and Spriggs felt that Amos would rest comfortably.

Spriggs left the lean-to and stood overlooking the camp for several minutes. Here he was, isolated halfway up a steep mountain pass, alone save for a mysterious, unconscious boy. Try as he might, he couldn't force himself to think about the future, about what would happen next. He was wrapped up in the events of the day, in the emotional carnage following the loss of a good friend. His reverie was broken by the flight of the curious jay into his camp. Landing on a log placed near the now cold campfire, the blue jay seemed to appraise Spriggs, cocking its head to one side, then another, while watching the miner. It took flight once again, soaring across the clearing and landing directly on the blanket-wrapped body of Wylie Morris. Fighting off the urge to toss a stone at the bird, Spriggs waited and watched as the inquisitive jay perched on the body, looked around the camp, and then soared straight up above the tall pines.

Looking on in wonder, Spriggs thought that perhaps the Indians were right. Perhaps animals did lead you to the afterlife. It gave him comfort to think of Morris's soul following the jay up, higher and higher, directly to the heavenly throne of Jesus Christ himself. Someday, Spriggs was now absolutely sure, he and Wylie Morris would meet again.

Spriggs walked to the open grave and stood there a moment, dreading the task before him. He moved Morris's body directly to the edge of the grave, then jumped into the four foot-deep hole. He reached for the blanket and began to pull the body into the grave.

"Easy there, lad," a gruff voice said.

Spriggs looked up over his shoulder in absolute shock. There above him stood an older man, short of stature and dressed in mountain man style. His huge .50 caliber rifle was pointed in Spriggs' general direction. His weathered buckskins were decorated with long, discolored fringes and his nut-brown face looked like the Judgement Day itself. Stern, stubbled and etched by wind, water and time, it was a face that allowed no room for doubt, no room for mercy.

Spriggs' mind reeled, trying to find something concrete to hold on to. He was a careful man, and he *had* been careful. He couldn't believe someone had gotten the drop on him. He had heard or sensed nothing, absolutely nothing.

Finally, he found his voice.

"Who're you?"

The mountain man backed up a step, not answering. "Haul yersef on outta there," he said. "We need to pow-wow awhile afore ye commit this'uns bones to the ground."

Backing up even more, the mountain man moved the barrel of the gun back and forth twice, silently ordering the miner from the grave. He backed up and allowed Spriggs to haul himself up and dust himself off.

Spriggs stood erect, a half-head taller than the mountain man, and stared in both wonder and annoyance.

"What's gone on here?" the mountain man asked, his eyes boring into the miner's.

Spriggs looked back at the man and, all of the sudden, he knew. He knew why he had heard nothing. He knew why even the birds seemed undisturbed. A spirit walks where it will, he reckoned, and neither man nor beast can feel it lest it wants to be known. He knew he was looking at Sam Tate. And with the realization came hope, the hope that the bandits who had killed Morris were on

139

the road to hell.

"You're Tate, ain't you?" he said.

"That I am."

"I heard about you, all right. Morris and me stayed a few days with Kate Patterson before we headed up here. Kate described you to a T. Said you was a ghost in the woods.

"I believe him, now."

"Morris, you say?" asked the mountain man.

"Yep, Wylie Morris. My friend whose burial you just interrupted."

Tate ignored the sarcasm, and thought for a moment. "That would make ye Spriggs, then, wouldn't it?"

"How do you know me?" the astonished miner asked.

"I don't," answered Tate. "But I make it my bidness to know who's crawlin' 'round *Cucharas* country.

"Kate told me ye boys'd dropped by a couple months back. Said ye was straight as arrows. Southern boys, like him."

"That we are," said Spriggs. He looked balefully at Morris's body and added, "Or were."

A look of pure venomous hate came over Tate's face as he looked at the body, then around the camp.

"Garcias, I'd swear," he stated. "Ye see 'em?"

"Fairly shot one of 'em, a young'un. Horse stepped in a hole just as I let go. I think I put a stripe down his neck, though.

"The older one shot Morris, here. Luckiest shot I ever seen."

"How so?"

"Well, he's hurtin'. Said he was shot in the arm. He still managed to twist around after his horse knocked me down and shoot Wylie as he dove for his pistol. Like I said, lucky shot."

Tate gave a noncommittal shrug.

"Tweren't no shot in his arm," he said. "One'a Gen'ral Carson's Ute scouts put a throwing knife in up to the hilt,

140

seems like."

He continued his inquiry.

"There's a boy was with 'em. Looks like they tied him to a tree yonder, but he walked away. Fell down the gorge into the river." Tate raised his eyebrows. "Somebody brung him back up.

"I don't know if'n he was shot, but there's a tree with a slug in it up the hill."

"That there is," said Spriggs. "Garcia missed, thank God. The boy jumped at just the right time."

"I was afraid yer partner here was him. Does he still live? Do ye have 'im?"

"I have him," answered Spriggs, who began to tell Tate the tale of the encounter with the outlaws and his rescue of the boy. He led the tracker up to the moment he'd been surprised when burying his partner. When he'd finished, he began walking toward the lean-to, leading Tate to the boy.

"By the way," Spriggs said, "what's his name?"

"Amos. Amos Herold. Pap's Jake Herold, down to the Crossin'."

"I know Jake," said the surprised Spriggs. "I bought supplies from him on my way south. Didn't see this boy here, though."

The two men approached the lean-to and pulled back the canvas cover on the north end, keeping quiet in order not to disturb the boy. Tate followed Spriggs into the small structure, his eyes adjusting to the dim light. He saw Spriggs' body tense as they looked around. A supply pack was laying in the corner next to a bedroll. Nothing else.

Amos Herold was gone!

The two men nearly tripped over one another running out of the structure, stumbling about and surveying the surrounding area. Tate immediately began following a set of unsteady scuffs on the ground, leading off toward the forest. Spriggs yelled from behind.

"He can't have been gone long. No more than ten minutes before you showed up."

Tate warily followed the trail of the boy, seeing no evidence that the Garcias had returned to kidnap him once more. He walked nearly a hundred yards through the thick pine forest, followed closely by Spriggs. At a junction where the pine forest thinned into an extended slope of stunning green aspen, Tate stopped and surveyed the area. He motioned for Spriggs to join him and then pointed. There, beneath an outcropping of lichen-encrusted rock, a brown boot was barely visible. Tate favored Spriggs with a grim smile, then whispered.

"Don't wanna shake the boy's sand. Wanna make him think he's still hid."

Tate and Spriggs stood for two or three minutes, listening to the sounds of the mountains—the cascading stream, the chattering birds, and even the deep, ever present and always mysterious moan of the high country wind through the craggy canyons. Then, with a controlled voice, Tate yelled to the boy.

"Amos Herold." His voice echoed through the mountain forest. "Don't fear, boy. It's Sam Tate."

The momentary silence seemed endless. All natural forest sounds ceased, as if the green foliage were holding its collective breath, waiting for an answer. Finally, a tired young voice broke the silence.

"Sam?"

"It's me, boy. Light and set. I'm here fer ye, boy!"

The men watched the boot slowly disappear into the forest, then heard the rustle of foliage being disturbed. Amos Herold appeared, haltingly making his way through the trees.

"Is it you, Sam?" he asked. "Really?"

"Yes, Amos, it's yer ol' pal Sam. C'mon here. Let's have a look at ye."

The boy stepped from behind two seemingly intertwined

aspens, looked suspiciously at the two waiting men, and then stumbled down the slope.

Tate grabbed the boy as he neared, inspected him briefly, then spoke.

"Let's head on back to camp, lad. I want to find out what's happened to ye."

"Yessir," said Amos, still dazed and uncommunicative.

Returning down the slope into camp, Tate's wary eyes constantly scanned the surrounding forest. Assessing no danger, they entered the camp and sat on logs near the cold ashes, then waited for Amos to talk.

"My Dad...?" he began, his questioning eyes on Tate.

"Jake'll be fine, lad. Took a bullet, but he's far too tough a man to kill." Chuckling, he added, "You know that.

"Yer mam and brothers are all fine, too.

"Now, this here's Narvel Spriggs. He's alive 'cause of ye. And, ye're alive 'cause of him.

"Now, Spriggs, I saw ye've a mule and a mare corralled to the west. I'd like to bring my hoss in fer a short spell."

With that, the mountain man disappeared into the forest. Spriggs took the time to question Amos, learning about the Garcias' killing of Tate's daughter and her family, and about the two assaults on Herold's Crossing. Five minutes later, Tate led the magnificent black into the clearing.

"Lancaster!" yelled Amos.

"Thought this might give ye a rise," chuckled Tate. "Borryed this big ol' hoss from yer mam, I did. My ol' Tom was tuckered out from the chase. Lancaster here 'n me 're gettin' used to each other—make a good team."

Tate led the horse through the clearing and over a shallow rise, disappearing momentarily before coming back alone minutes later. He sat facing Amos as he prepared a pipe of tobacco, offering some to Spriggs. When the miner declined, Tate merely shrugged his shoulders, produced a long match which burst into flame when he flicked it against his fingernail, and lit the pipe.

Now he was ready.

Tate quickly gave Amos a bare bones report on the battle at Herold's Crossing. The boy listened in wonder, wide-eyed. Finally, when Tate had finished, Amos told them about his abduction and of how he witnessed the killing of Vivian Garcia. Tate interjected that the outlaw was killed by Lieutenant Homer Keating, who was on the trail a few hours behind Tate, along with two Ute scouts, and Billy Carson and Kate Patterson.

Amos continued, relating his bone-jarring ride to the foothills, then the forced march up the pass. He told of being tied by his hands to the large branch, and of breaking the small one with his weight on the rope. Finally, he told of warning the miners, and of seeing Filipio Garcia aim his rifle.

"My only choice was to jump down the canyon, Sam. I remember rollin' and rollin', then the freezin' water. Next thing I knew, Mr..."

"Spriggs," interjected Tate.

"...Spriggs here, was carrying me into the lean-to yonder. I pretended to be asleep so I could make a plan in private."

"Why'd ye run, boy?" asked Tate.

"I didn't know not to. I was confused and thought maybe the Garcias were still here. When I heard the quiet, and just two voices talking, I crawled to the door and looked about. I couldn't see anyone, so I slipped out the other side and took off.

"Didn't get far, though, did I?"

"Ye did fine, son. Now, we need to figger out where to go from here. But fust, they's somethin' needs attendin', right Spriggs?"

Spriggs solemnly nodded and stood. Tate did the same and helped Amos up, holding on to the unsteady boy's arm as the group made its way across the clearing to the gravesite.

Amos looked at the shrouded form lying next to the grave and said, "Your partner?"

"Yep," answered Spriggs. "A fine partner he was."

"I'm sorry, Mr. Spriggs. I wish I could have gotten loose sooner—done something to help."

"Oh, you did help, boy, you did. I'll carry Wylie's mem'ry with me fer a good long time. As long as I'm still kickin', I'll see that he's not forgotten."

Tate guided Amos to a tree trunk and sat him against it. Then he returned and helped Spriggs maneuver Morris's body into the grave. Spriggs jumped into the hole and laid the body out gently on the bottom. Gratefully, he grabbed Tate's outstretched hand and scrambled out of the grave.

The two stood above the body, and were silent, thinking their own thoughts. Spriggs nervously cleared his throat a couple of times, then began.

"I don't know the words to send Wylie here on his way. Wish I did but I don't. All I know is that he was a true *compadre* and a fine man. I think the Lord God and his holy son Jesus Christ have a good new partner in heaven."

"Amen to that," said Tate. He added, "From the wind and the water and the earth we come. To the wind and the water and the earth we return."

As the two men shoveled dirt into the hole, the watching boy leaned back against the tree, gave a great sigh that served to stifle his tears, and muttered to himself, "Ashes to ashes, dust to dust."

Filipio Garcia tried unsuccessfully to purge the events at the miners' camp from his mind. He knew that anger was unproductive, but he could not completely stem the tide of absolute fury that seemed to be crushing his chest.

He rode up a narrow game trail with Santiago closely behind. For the past two hours, he had to almost physically restrain himself from pulling his pistol, turning around and blowing the idiot boy's head from his body. He enjoyed playing with the mental image, seeing the fire spit from the gun, seeing the shock in the boy's eyes a split second before there were no eyes left. It was a compelling image, and Filipio had to remind himself that it must continue to be just an image for the time being. But soon, very soon...

The horses kept climbing through the hottest part of the day. Pushed to their limit, they desperately required rest and water, but Garcia could not give them the luxury. He survived by his wits, by utilizing surprise, and by a generally reliable sense of the order of things. In reasoning the probabilities of his situation, he realized he might be better off than he thought. The boy had escaped but was surely dead from the great fall he had taken. But the miner, the one who had survived, was certainly on his way to get help. But what kind of help? The men from Herold's Crossing were no doubt on his trail, but what of Sam Tate? Was the old mountain man with them, or did he come alone? Did he even come at all?

He survived on suppositions, and he presumed that pursuit was coming, yet they had to be far behind, and he had taken great care to hide the trail from the miners' camp. They could probably be in Antonito or San Luis within two days, and from there disappear for awhile until it was time to strike again. Yet, there was always Tate to reckon with.

Working out the logistics of his situation calmed him somewhat and allowed him to even experience a sense of visceral excitement. He was on the run, a bad *hombre,* taking what he wanted. Surely children were coaxed to bed at night through the use of his name. He laughed at the thought, in his mind conjuring up a gruff father shouting at his child, sounding much like his own father. *Listen, you get to bed or Filipio Garcia's gonna come to get ya, ya hear?*

Although he had lost young Herold, who seemed to be a perfect hostage, through Santiago's stupidity and inability to do something as simple as tie a rope properly, he still managed to take solace in the fact that he had made a magnificent shot to kill the miner. If only the rifle hadn't jammed, he would have killed the other one and taken the food and supplies they so desperately needed.

As for Santiago, he knew that he might need the boy if trouble was to follow. But after they reached the Sandias, his body would be found tied to a giant *cholla* cactus, his blood slowly seeping into the ground.

As he mused, his exhausted horse began to stumble every few steps. Halting, he painfully jumped down and inspected his mount's hooves, looking for an irritating stone. He found nothing, and realized that the horse was nearly dead on its feet. It had been run hard since the fight at Herold's Crossing, and even before. It either needed rest, or he needed a new horse.

Santiago rode up behind his uncle and sat silently, his stirruped feet thrusting in and out from his spent horse's sides in time to its ragged breathing.

Filipio looked up at his mounted nephew and motioned him down. Santiago did not respond and continued to sit on the near dead horse.

Filipio made a mental promise to make sure Santiago would be in great pain when tied to the cactus. Then, he spoke to the boy in a reassuring manner.

"We will walk for awhile, and lead the horses back through the thickest part of the trees, where no man can track us. Perhaps not even the spirit, Tate. We'll rest and search for food."

"Then what?" asked the boy, contempt in his tone. "Do we run some more?"

Garcia's eyes smoldered as he fought to control his temper.

"It is not I who runs from men and guns, nephew," he said curtly, "it is you. Now, do we play silly women's games, or do you dismount and follow?"

147

Santiago indulged himself in another moment of rebellion, then slowly slipped from the saddle and onto the pine needle covered ground.

Garcia took a long look at his nephew, reluctantly decided not to kill him then and there, then turned around to start up the slope, into a heavily forested hill on the south side of the pass.

Soon, they were surrounded by shimmering aspen growing in the thin soil. An abundance of hard, lichen-covered granite helped to hide their progress from tracker's eyes, although Filipio knew that a spirit such as Tate could follow. He hoped to find a brook or small stream up ahead that could be be used to disguise their movements. If they could find such a brook, they would enter its current and walk down its center for some distance, hopefully obliterating their trail completely.

They continued through the aspen grove, ascending a rise that seemed to top out three or four hundred yards ahead. Garcia pushed himself, fighting the incredible pain in his arm. They would rest when they reached the hill's summit, he told himself.

He led the stumbling horse nearer to the top of the rise, when a far-off noise floated through the air. He stopped and held the reins in his right hand straight up, halting his horse and his nephew behind him. He listened closely and heard only the breeze blowing through the multitude of small canyons. Then he heard it again.

The bellow of a bull!

He quickly scrambled up the rise. As he reached the top, he looked down in wonder at a beautiful small valley. A stream banked by willows ran through its center, the long, green grass on either side forming a good-sized meadow. Although not a man to recognize beauty, Filipio Garcia did recognize opportunity. Surveying the scene before him, he smiled and began to descend.

The valley below was dotted with cattle.

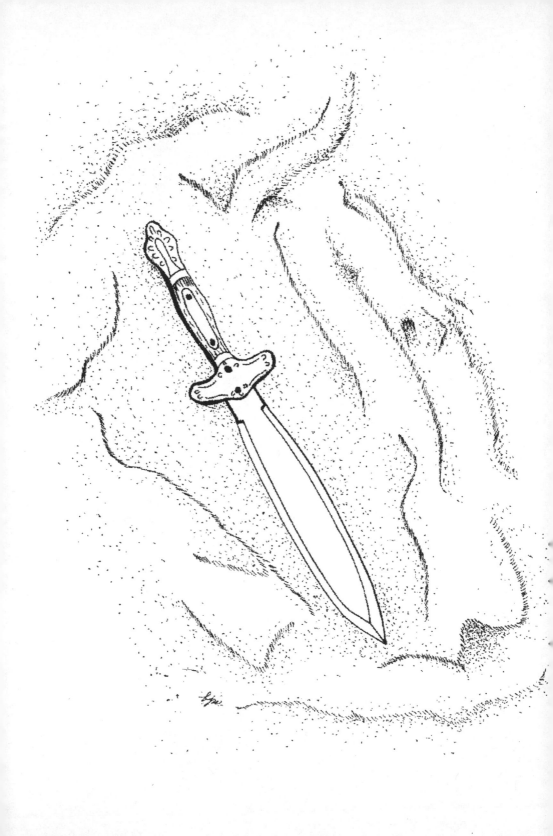

*"...carvings on the dull metal handle
began to emerge."*

CHAPTER TEN

"I WANT TO COME WITH YOU, SAM."

Amos Herold had thought long and hard about how to
approach Sam Tate with his request. In the end, he figured
being blunt was the only way to proceed.

He felt as if he'd been, as their family friend Hiram
Vasquez often said, "et by a wolf that was et by a bear." He
was so stiff and sore, it hurt to move. Yet, he somehow
knew he had begun a significant passage. He would only
find out where it led him if he continued down the path.
He was not surprised that he wanted to go, needed to go.
At thirteen, he had already shot a man, admittedly a bad
man, but a man nonetheless. He had saved the life of
another. He knew that he had to see this thing through.

Tate had been securing rawhide riggings to Lancaster
and was testing the saddle to make sure it was tight. Amos
approached him, and when close enough to summon suf-
ficient courage, blurted out to Tate what was on his mind.
The tracker looked at the young boy, snorted and shook
his head sideways.

"Naw, son, ain't no way. Ye come outta the lion's den
onct, awready. I ain't about to send ye back in.

"Besides, ye look like ye bin hoss-whipped, boy."

Amos did indeed look as if he'd been lashed. His wrists

151

were rubbed raw and bloody from being bound, and he had long, deep scratches down his face, the result of wheeling through branches during his fall. He had virtually no skin left on his elbows and knees, and one palm was a bloody mess. His finger was broken and he limped. Yet, he wanted to go.

Tate shook his head and chuckled, his heart full of respect for the young man who was, by the mountain man's reckoning, a boy no longer.

"Sam, I want to come," Amos continued. "I think that somehow, I *have* to come. You'll need someone to calm Lancaster here, to hold him and quiet him while you're checking out trails.

"I won't be a burden Sam. I'm bruised up, but I can hold my own, I reckon."

Amos was quiet for a moment, then haltingly continued.

"Sam, they shot my Dad and they tried to kill me. And Sam, you know how much Johnny 'n me got along. I *got* to come with you, Sam."

Tate nearly winced at the thought of his grandson, but he remembered the way John Gorner idolized Amos Herold. Only three years separated them, and Amos was more of a big brother to Johnny than anything else. In his mind, he could still see the two boys running around the barn at Jed and Emily's spread, laughing loud enough to scare the crows from the trees.

The sound of the ever present breeze was accompanied only by Lancaster's soft neigh and the whipping of his tail in an attempt to scatter deer flies. Tate stood with his weight on one leg and was quiet, his mind considering the situation. Once again, his instinct took over, filling him with an intuitive certainty he could only identify as *right*. He had followed this instinct throughout his whole life, and reasoned that he should do it once again. In so deciding, he did something he swore he would never do—put the life of a young one in danger.

"Yeer pap'll have my hide, but I do understand, boy.

"I'll take ye along, but it ain't as a favor. I figure mebbe I *do* need someone to tend that big ol' hoss. I could rightly use a young pair of eyes, too, I figger.

"Besides, I ain't never laid eyes on them murderin' dogs. I need ye to describe 'em, right down to they eyebrows if'n ye can."

Amos nearly jumped for joy, prevented only by the fact that doing so would have been impossible in his condition. He rapidly reminded himself of the danger inherent in the trip and curbed his impulses. In fact, he finally allowed himself the fear which the pursuit of the Garcias would cause. At 13, he was learning that facing fear squarely was the only way to conquer it.

"Mr. Morris won't be needin' that hoss o' his agin in this life," said Tate. "I 'spect Spriggs'll part with 'im fer a day or two."

Spriggs seemed surprised that Tate was allowing the boy to go along on the hunt for the desperados, but seeing the determination in Amos's face, he realized that he would probably just take off after Tate anyway. Honoring Tate's request, the miner fetched his dead partner's horse, secured the saddle, and adjusted the stirrups to fit Amos's legs. He filled Morris's pack with essentials and rolled it up in a bedroll that was tied behind the saddle.

Spriggs lastly set to work building a fire and cooking over it.

"Cain't let you boys take off hungry," he said. "Might be some time before you eat again."

After the meal, Tate thanked Spriggs and made a promise to return the horse. Spriggs had decided to continue mining the promising area, and would wait for word from Tate before riding either west to Fort Garland or east to Francisco's Fort in order to send Morris's effects to his family in Georgia. Tate felt that Homer Keating and his party would likely be along in the next few hours, with

Kate Patterson among them. The news that Morris had been killed would be hard on his fellow Georgian, but he would certainly aid Spriggs in finding Morris's survivors.

Finally, Tate and Amos mounted the horses and bade goodbye to Spriggs. As they started up the trail taken by the Garcias hours earlier, Tate spoke softly but sternly to Amos. "Amos Herold, my word is law. If we're ten miles up the hill and I change my mind, ye'll turn 'round and come back with nary a word. Understood?"

"Yessir," answered Amos. He then fell into a deep silence, feeling each step of the horse jolt his abused body, and silently trying to counter the pain.

Watching Tate work was an astonishing education for Amos. The mountain man seemed to enter a trance as they followed the outlaws' trail. Often, he would raise his hand, signalling Amos to rein in his horse, while he sat in the saddle for minutes at a time, looking around before taking off one direction or another. The boy was too tired to question Tate about his methods and often felt absolutely lost in the wilderness. Then, out of nowhere, Tate would point out a barely-broken branch or a hoofprint, or fly-covered horse droppings laying between two trees. Somehow, Tate was finding small signs and reading them, following the outlaws' trail as if it were on a map in front of him.

Twice, Tate silently dropped from his mount and disappeared into the pines, only to return minutes later from a different direction. Each time, he grabbed Lancaster's reins and walked him through a gap in the foliage, motioning for Amos to stay. The boy waited patiently until the man and horse returned and indicated for him to follow.

As they progressed, the land slowly became much more vertical. Forested hills seemed to reach straight to the sky, while on the north slope of the pass, broad stretches of sage were interspersed between pinon pines and low lying junipers. The diffused light of the late afternoon seemed to turn the area into an enchanted place, like something out of one of the books his mother still kept in her cedar trunk. Amos found himself looking toward those vast, yet contained expanses, imagining that no man had ever traversed them. Yet, he knew that ancient eyes in ancient times had gazed upon these mountains, and that Ute warriors even now passed silently through the land. Still, he wondered what urgent need possessed men to push on, to travel through and claim country that was so large, so impressive. He felt that need in himself now, a need to both play out the drama that was unfolding and at the same time see what was over the next hill. The land was intriguing, he realized, and its beauty was addictive. He thought it was so beautiful that it could probably cause madness. Someday, he thought, he would live in this place, on this magnificent pass. Someday.

After three hours of patient travel, the pair was carefully following a slender natural bench on the south grade of the pass. Tate suddenly halted Amos and turned around to talk.

"Trail leads pretty near straight up here fer awhile. I'm gonna scout it some, make sure them divils ain't holed up 'n ready to bushwhack us."

The tracker looked up at the sky and judged the time, then lightly touched the boy's horse on the nose, gently soothing it.

"Why'nt ye give this'n a rest? I'll be a quarter hour or so. Keep yerself hid, Amos, 'n outten the line a fire."

Before disappearing on foot for a third time, Tate helped Amos pull himself from his horse and walk to a depression between two pines. An uprooted tree had rolled down the steep grade, resting against the trunks of two solidly rooted trees, forming a natural barricade. To the left, several other fallen trees had rolled down the mountainside, scattering brush and exposing granite. Looking back up the grade, Amos could see where a piece of ridge had given way, probably during a heavy downpour, and had

155

caused the damage below.

Amos sat in the cover of the depression, nursing his aches and pains, and resting as best he could. His horse was picketed within sight, in the deep shadows of a stand of spruce. The panorama below him was stunning, and he feasted his eyes. To the far side of the pass, he saw the movement of several deer, carefully picking their way through the edge of the forest in preparation for their trip down to water and forage in the early evening. He saw several eagles and even more crows fly out over the expanse, as well as blue jays and camp robbers. Several pines stripped of bark at their highest levels testified to the presence of porcupines.

The beauty in front of him was enhanced by long shadows as the sun sank slowly lower in the west. The impending dusk made him drowsy, and he fought sleep by going over and over the events of the past hours, the most momentous of his life. In an effort to stay awake, he began carefully studying zones in front of him, taking a section of land and making sure nothing within was disturbed by the passing of the Garcias, or worse yet by their presence. As the shadows imperceptibly lengthened, he noticed that one of the uprooted trees some thirty yards below had jammed against a shale-like outcropping. The quartz- and mica-imbedded granite had weathered over the years, and a large, flat slab from the top of the formation had been driven by the tree's force into a leaning position over the rest of the outcropping. The force of the tree's collision had caused stones and debris to cascade down the hill, where rushing water had gathered much of it in a flat, granite bowl.

Amos eyed the odd formation for a full minute, sensing that something was not quite right. Finally, he noticed that the shadows appeared deeper under the leaning slab of stone, like the entrance to a mine or tunnel. Moving painfully, he slowly crawled down the slope toward the formation. As he approached, he noticed that the deep shadow was indeed an entrance of some sort, leading back into the hillside beneath the granite formation. The available light was diffused through the trees, offering thin shafts of brightness that penetrated the quickly darkening shadows. Amos could now see where brush and a long dead tree trunk had covered the entrance to what seemed to be a low, shallow cavern formed under the granite outcropping. The recent deluge from above had apparently stripped the foliage and uprooted the trunk, exposing part of the entrance to the open.

After checking the surrounding area for tracks to make sure no one had recently approached the area, Amos slowly bent to peek into the depression, which was perhaps ten feet in width and seemed to extend back into the wall some fifteen to twenty feet. As his eyes adjusted, he saw that the floor of the area was strewn with broken slabs of granite and a few boulders. He entered the blackness and sat for a moment, closing his eyes to let his sight acclimate completely to the dim light. When he reopened them, he saw that ground squirrel nests dotted the area, and a hollowed out depression toward the rear seemed to indicate that a bear had wintered there in the recent past.

Seeing that the Garcias had not found and utilized the cleft in the granite, he began to inch back out toward the entrance. As he turned, he braced his hand against what he thought was a stone. It moved easily and had little weight, so he quickly removed his hand to study it. Holding the object up into a shaft of light that entered the opening, he brushed at the crusted dirt and dust covering it and saw that it appeared to be some sort of wood and metal contraption. He turned it around in his hands, and then recognized it for what it was—a short musket. The wooden handle was in bad shape, brittle and rotting, but the metal frame still had substantial areas that would likely shine up with a little elbow grease.

His heart rapidly pounding, Amos Herold realized that the musket was old, very old. He laid it aside and looked once more to the rear of the depression, surveying the ground once more. He reached out and grabbed what he thought was merely a tree branch and discovered that he was holding a smooth bone. Not part of a deer or elk skeleton, but a different bone, large and long. He felt it almost tingling in his hands as he came to the conclusion that it must be human, a leg bone no doubt. Looking carefully around, he saw that several bones of differing sizes were scattered about. It struck him that he was looking at the remains of a human, a man or woman who had died in this place. He had managed to stumble across a large natural crypt, obviously violating its sanctity for the first time in many years.

He then stared intently at one of the large rocks in the rear of the depression. His heart pounded wildly as he realized that the stones were something much different than he had first realized. Frantically brushing dust and debris away, he unearthed a metal breastplate. Forged to a peak running vertically, the armor had rotten leather straps running through grommets in the two flanges that protected the shoulders. He gently brushed the caked dirt away from the edges and picked it up. Underneath, scraps of tattered red cloth covered more bones, those that had not been scattered by varmints, no doubt.

Probing further he discovered a long sword, its hilt ornately carved. He lifted it and tried to pull it from its sheath, but couldn't make it budge.

Knowing full well what was coming next, Amos carefully put the sword aside and reached for a large object above the breastplate. Steeling himself, he uncovered a smooth, slightly rusted metal helmet. The crested helmet had wide wings encasing it, coming to a peak in the front. Connected to it was another dirt encrusted object. As he lifted the helmet, the human skull separated and rested in the boy's hands. He set aside the helmet and lifted the skull to the shaft of light. Scraps of reddish-blond hair were still connected. He looked deep into the sockets, his emotions overwhelming him. Fear, wonder and discovery combined as he pondered the remains.

"What happened to you?" he whispered to the skull. "Why are you here? *Who are you?"*

"Conquistadore," a familiar voice answered.

Amos let out a short yelp as his head snapped back toward the cavity's entrance. There, making sure not to block what little light entered the hole, knelt Sam Tate. His voice had echoed in the enclosed area, causing Amos's heart to nearly burst through his chest.

Amos had heard nothing of Tate's approach. Even the light was not disturbed. He realized that the stories told about Tate were true. Perhaps he was a spirit, after all.

"Aw, Sam, you scared the devil outta me," he sputtered, his heart continuing to beat wildly.

Tate silently entered the cavity, siding up next to Amos. He gestured and Amos handed him the skull. He looked it over with a grim smile.

"Whaugh. Mightn't be a bad idee fer them Garcias to come to this end," he said flatly.

He gently set the skull down and, while carefully looking over the other ancient effects, talked to Amos about the discovery.

"Ye've got yerself a Spanish warrior here, lad. A *conquistadore,* a conqueror, ye know, an adventurer."

"Conquistadore?" queried Amos.

"Yep. I heered they was some 'a these boys got up near Pikes Peak way 'n mebbe even futher on. Spanish Peaks, the *Huajatolla,* are named fer the Spanyerds. Seems like this'un here crawled into a hole to die. No marks on his armor, so's it was likely some ailment what kilt him.

"I seen things like this down Santa Fe way, but never this far north. From the looks, I'd say this 'ol boy was an officer, awright. Mebbe one 'a Coronado's."

Tate leaned over and brushed the debris from an unrecognizable lump. A long double-edged dagger took shape, nearly a short sword, specked with spots of rust and dirt. He rubbed it for a moment, and carvings on the dull metal handle began to emerge.

"This dry air'll keep things, Amos," he said. "Heck, down to the Mississippi there'd be no leather still strapped to that there armor. This knife'd be nothin' but a lump'a rust. But it's in fine shape, it is. A little elbow grease..." he trailed off.

Amos looked in wonder at the artifacts, losing all thought of the horror of the past days and of their mission, as well. It was up to Tate to bring him back to the present.

"I'd say you made quite a discov'ry here, lad. Now, were it me, I'd like as not try to roll yonder tree tight against the mouth 'a this wee cave, and let the 'ol boy continue his eternal rest."

Amos looked at the mountain man uneasily, and started to speak. He was interrupted by Tate.

"Whatever ye do, son, ye'll have to do later. We got precious little light, and I think I know where to find them divils. We got to go now so's I kin position myself proper."

Amos thought for a moment, then held out his hand. Tate handed him the knife with the etched handle that had lain so long with the Spaniard's remains.

"Sam, you're right. Let's leave him be. But do you think he'd miss this knife? I'd like to keep it to show people I'm not a liar."

Tate looked at the boy, stifled a grin, and said, "Naw, I spect he's lost all use fer sech earthly instruments."

Tate and Amos scrambled from the small cave and stood. Darkness was less than an hour away, and Tate obviously wanted to be gone. But before they walked upslope to the horses, he grabbed an uprooted sapling and, using it as a lever, rolled the tree that had displaced the outcropping's overhanging slab into place in front of the opening.

"Nothing or nobody'll git in there now, Amos. Yeer Spaniard's secrets is safe."

"I'll come back here some day," said Amos, wistfully looking at the ancient crypt. The extraordinary day had entered the realm of disbelief, and he could not comprehend it all.

"That ye will, boy. That ye will."

As they mounted and took off on the outlaws' trail, Tate explained what he'd found. A few hundred yards up the slope, the outlaws had taken to some thick foliage in an attempt to lose pursuit. A little farther on, they had started walking, likely to rest horses that had been abused since the murders of Jed, Emily and John Gorner.

"I've a good mind where they's headed," said Tate. "Yonder four or five miles is a little hidden valley where a coupla ol' companyeros 'a mine bin runnin' cattle fer the past coupla years. It's surrounded close by tight trees, keepin' the cows outta the forest. Plenty 'a water and grass, if'n I remember straight.

"They's access from below, and a reg'ler trail runnin' on the other side'a the pass. I 'spect them divils think they have a lead that can't be beat. They's gunmen, and not men 'a the land. They'll wanna stop 'n rest awhile where they's water 'n food.

"Now, I could foller 'em on in, but I've another plan. There's few clouds and a full moon, so we kin travel. We'll skirt the valley, cross over to the north side 'a the Saddle here. I figger 'bout fifteen, twenty miles 'a ridin'. I plan to come at 'em where they expect it least. From the west."

The mountain man spoke slowly as the horses carefully picked their way through the thick forest.

"'Course, any plan can be busted, lad. Could be they skirted the valley theyselves. Or they mighta just rode on through, lookin' fer more miners or cowboys to rob and kill. If they's still movin', we'll cut back to they trail 'an pick it up agin.

"But I 'spect they stopped," he said grimly.

Despite the receding light, Amos could plainly see Tate's face. The high cheekbones and berry brown eyes seemed of Indian origin, indeed, but the fair hair and aristocratic nose spoke of Irish or Scottish roots. It was a face seemingly carved in stone, etched with hate and despair. It was the face of someone whose eyes could not be closed, of someone who was forever vigilant.

By Amos's reckoning, Tate could have had no sleep in nearly two full days, yet he was awake and aware. If he was tired, he kept it to himself. Amos, on the other hand, began drifting in and out of sleep as the horses ambled down the slope and toward the midpoint—the Saddle—of La Veta Pass.

Tate looked back at the boy periodically and, seeing Amos was desperate to remain awake, reached into his possibles sack and pulled out a palm-sized whetstone. "Here," he said as he handed the stone to the boy. "Work that thar Spaniard's knife with this. Should hold an edge by the look of it."

Amos took the whetstone and wrapped his horse's reins around the saddle's pommel, allowing his mount to follow Tate's without guidance. He pulled the ancient dagger from a saddlebag and began to sharpen the knife's edges, quickly learning to move the stone and knife together in time with his horse's gait. Within minutes, he could see bright metal gleaming through the grime. Surprisingly, the knife was made of good steel, indeed.

The boy had undergone much, Tate thought, and would undergo even more before things were said and done. He was a fine, strong boy, much like Johnny Gorner.

Thinking of Johnny, a great melancholy came over Tate. As he rode to the northwest in order to skirt the small valley, he allowed himself to think of the past few days, and of their impact on the lives of his friends and family. He knew that nothing could be helped, that the Garcias had entered their lives merely by chance, but he was resentful and furious nonetheless.

Chance had made up so much of his life. It was by chance that he traveled to the West, and by chance that he found Bright Star. It was by chance again that he met and courted Esther in St. Louis, and it was chance that brought them darling little Emily.

God, he thought, Emily. His heart was truly broken. From the first time he laid eyes on her as a prisoner in the Kiowa camp, he knew she was special. Even as a toddler, her wit was as striking as her beauty, and when her frail and fragile mother died, he and Esther welcomed her into their family. Emily and Mary were inseparable, rarely remembering that they were not sisters by blood, but by fortune. In fact, the few people who knew of Emily's past either forgot or pretended to, and the girls thought it was no one's business.

To lose her this way was inconceivable. To lose Johnny was even more so. He often thought that passion dimmed with age, but the rage and anguish her murder inspired in his soul was as vivid and real as any emotion in his life. It drove him and inspired him, at the same time it drained him. Yet, he didn't know if he would wish it away if he were given the chance. The conviction he held seemed to validate his loss. His mission was to destroy, not in order to make things right, but to apply vengeance in all its terrible equality. Lives were taken. Their killers would die. It was that simple.

He sought revenge. His black rage and his red blood required it. And while he knew it would not bring Emily or Johnny or Jed back, it would serve to salve some superficial wounds, and in the end, to verify justice.

Yet, he still could not shake the resentment he felt toward an existence that at times seemed nothing more than a long, anxious gamble. In fact, he could think of little in his life that resulted from concrete planning. As a trapper, tracker and mountain man, his life could not be static, but rather held possibilities for adventure and the unexpected. At one time in his life, he told himself he loved surprises; that he'd rather have a mountain cat come at him from time to time than to sit in a rocking chair surveying the scenery. These days, he changed his mind. He hated surprises.

He was jolted from his thoughts by the distinctive yipping of a coyote as the last light of day slipped beyond the peaks. His frontier-honed ears authenticated the sound, judging the call to be a small wolf's rather than the eerily similar imitation peculiar to many Indian tribes. He thought of the many times such uncanny discrimination of sounds had saved his life, and he waited for the dog to howl once again before resting easy. He desperately wanted no surprises now. He had not factored Utes into the mix, and would welcome them only if they managed to capture the Garcias and skin them alive.

Tate continued to check on Amos as the moon rose above, illuminating the pass. The rough, swirling sound of the Spaniard's dagger rubbing against the whetstone was strangely reassuring, and Tate smiled to himself each time he looked back at the boy.

Guiding the horses with precision, Tate led them up next to the tree line, moving from shadow to shadow as they ascended the pass.

Five hours later, Tate led two horses and a drowsy boy into a small clearing concealed by an aspen grove. He slipped from the saddle and picketed Lancaster, then walked over to gently wake Amos.

The boy's eyes were already open and surveying the scene, and his hands were clasped securely around the whetstone and dagger. Aspen trunks shone silvery in the moonlight, contrasting with a million moving shadows caused by their fluttering leaves.

"Where are we, Sam?" asked Amos.

"On the west side 'a the little valley," answered Tate. "We bin quiet, boy, and I ain't heered a peep. If them divils is down below, I'll find 'em afore dawn. If not, we'll back-track through the valley and ketch their trail from there."

The boy looked sleepily at the mountain man before stretching his pain-wracked body and roughly sliding from his saddle to the ground.

"Do you think they're there?" he asked after he had caught his breath.

"Oh, yes, Amos lad. I think they're there," said Tate as he rolled a blanket out in the shadows. He reached into a pack.

"We'll make a dry camp here. Amos, I want ye to lay on down and rest a coupla hours. I'm goin' down the ridge yonder to have a peek into the valley—get my bearin's afore I sneak down at first light."

Before Amos could answer, Tate vanished like a ghost in the night. Once again, the boy marveled at the silent command over nature that Tate exercised. Perhaps he truly could track wind over water.

Within a half-hour Tate returned, only to find that Amos had not dozed off. He was sitting with his back against a tree, warily watching the moonlit landscape. Tate softly cleared his throat to avoid startling Amos and walked into the clearing.

"Light an shadow's dancin' too much down there. But I smell fire and cooked meat. Can't be my companyeros, either. They's over to Fort Garland."

Amos nodded his head in understanding.

"While you were gone, I thought I heard some cattle calling," he said.

"That ye did. Looks like a fine herd. Plenty 'a meat fer hungry *pistoleros.*"

Amos was quiet for a moment, pondering something.

Finally, he spoke in an almost apologetic manner.

"Sam, I don't have a gun."

"Naw, ye don't," answered the tracker. "But I slipped Morris's long rifle along."

He strode to Jake Herold's stallion and pulled the blanket covered rifle from a leather sheath.

"If he'd 'a kept this nearby, he'd like as not be minin' gold come mornin'," he said as he handed the rifle to Amos.

"Now ye hold on to it. I'm not countin' on ye needin' it, but ye'll never know. Should somethin' go wrong, ye hightail it outta the way to the north and keep yer eyes open fer Homer Keating, Billy Carson and them. They'll be along shortly, I 'spect, but I cain't afford to wait."

Amos nearly questioned Tate, nearly asked him why he couldn't wait. But the memory of Johnny's funeral and his own wounded father lying on the ground stopped him. Finally, he spoke.

"Sam, I got this rifle now. You take this Spaniard's knife. You never know when you might need a good knife, Sam."

Tate knelt in the shadows near Amos and nearly cracked a smile. "Ye're right, Amos, a good knife is a handy thing, it tis. Thankee, son. I'll take care of it fer ye."

Tate opened his buckskin jacket and slipped the knife into a loop on the belt around his waist. He then turned to Amos.

"Amos, it's important that the horses don't kick up, son. We'll keep 'em saddled so's they don't git too frisky. But they cain't neigh nor bray. They cain't do nothing but chew on grass.

"Now, they'll smell the water down below, and want to make tracks down to the stream. Ye need to be here if'n they get restless. Calm 'em. Sooth 'em. Slug 'em if'n ye have to. But don't let 'em yowl.

"I'm countin' on ye, lad."

Amos Herold thought that he had never heard finer words.

"The young outlaw was nearly 250 yards across the meadow..."

CHAPTER ELEVEN

SANTIAGO GARCIA AWOKE with a start. He had been dreaming of riding a fast horse, riding from something. But the dream evaporated the moment his eyes opened.

He had been nudged by a boot, and although it was still dark, the night was bright enough to see Filipio standing above him.

"Get up," Filipio Garcia said. "We have much to do and must go soon."

The boy grunted and sat up, his fatigue evident. He had not envisioned being a pistolero to be so exhausting. The pretty girls he had dreamed of never materialized, nor did all the gold. He had killed one small boy and run in fear from two gunfights. All he gained from his short career as an outlaw was a painful crease on his neck from a miner's bullet. Now, Vivian was gone, and he was left with his mad dog uncle, a man who believed in nothing. He had thought often of killing Filipio and surrendering, claiming that he had been forced to ride with his uncles. But he knew he would never be believed, and all that waited at the end of that road was a bullet or a noose. Instead he decided to ride with Filipio, hoping that the plan to reach San Luis was a good one. From there he would disappear, traveling south to Mexico, maybe joining the army.

The birds began their cacophony an hour before the first light shone to the east. Finches, sparrows, robins, and jays all began their distinctive calls, waking the valley, preparing it for the sun's arrival. The young outlaw knew time was short, so he jumped up and began saddling the two horses. Water and grass had helped them, but not much. They were still nearly dead on their feet, and would not last through the upcoming run. The outlaws' only chance was to come upon another mining camp or a ranch and steal fresh horses.

Filipio Garcia looked at his nephew with disgust and returned to packing his saddlebag. He knew this stop had allowed any pursuit to get much closer, but there had been no other choice. The horses would have died within hours of discovering the valley, and he had counted on the presence of cowboys running the herd, from whom horses could be stolen. He was shocked when he found no men in the valley, then realized that the thick forest formed a natural barrier that kept the cattle from escaping. Besides, the grass was lush and there was plenty of water. Aside from a possible wolf or coyote attack, the cattle were perfectly safe and out of danger.

After descending into the valley and carefully scouting the area, the outlaws had allowed their horses to approach the stream and drink. Filipio noticed a small structure set back in the pines and approached it on foot. After careful reconnaissance, he found that no one occupied the line shack. He contemplated breaking the lock with the butt of his rifle, but felt that the jarring would be too painful for his wounded arm. Finally, he viciously kicked the door, shattering the soft pine boards, and entered, finding little more than branding gear and various pieces of hardware. He grabbed a long, razor-sharp butcher knife from a table and went back outside. Remounting his exhausted horse, he once again scouted the area to make sure there were no people in the vicinity, then chose a fat steer grazing near where the stream entered the meadow and shot the animal. The echo of the discharge startled Santiago, who pulled his weapon and began dashing for cover. Thankfully, he heard Filipio's yell and joined him in preparing the steer for butchering.

By the time it was dark, Filipio had supervised Santiago as he used a rope pulled by the young outlaw's horse to hang the carcass over a stout tree limb. Using the sturdy knife, they quartered it and prepared fresh slabs of meat over a small fire hidden within a circle of thick pines. The branches and needles above dissipated the smoke, while nothing could dissipate the outlaws' ravenous appetites.

Throughout the night, while Santiago slept, Filipio continued cooking meat in preparation for the long ride ahead. He stopped only for an hour to rest, then resumed. As the sky imperceptibly lightened to the east, he nudged his nephew roughly with his boot. Now, thought Filipio, the idiot was up and about and could help break camp.

As Filipio Garcia watched Santiago saddle the horses, he began thinking of the ride ahead. The horses would not go far, of that he was sure. So, they would have to travel slowly and hope to run into someone with mounts they could steal. As he thought more about the plan, he realized it was as lame as the horses would be in a few miles.

Then it struck him. Here they sat with food and water. Why should they move? They stood a better chance of survival if they could rig some sort of trap. Surely, he could find a position to pick off those who chased them as they entered the valley. He figured there would be no more than three or four. Jake Herold was shot, so there would be only the army man and his Indians, no doubt. And perhaps Sam Tate. He thought they had probably stopped at the miners' camp for some time to find the Herold boy's body, so he must still have time.

He rose to call Santiago to brief him on the plan and to search for a hiding spot from which to ambush the pursuers. Then, like a flash, he realized that he might well kill two birds with one stone. He needed to convince Santiago to lead both horses out of the valley, drawing any pursuit after him. The trackers would follow, thinking both he and Santiago were riding. By the time they had caught and killed Santiago, he would either be hidden away in the mountains with plenty of food and water, or perhaps even be riding in another direction should luck present itself and he was able to kill one of the pursuers and take his horse. Either way, he could see no downside.

Although desperate and deadly, Filipio truly did not want to die. There were more desirable women to violate, other unfortunate men to kill, other fiery whiskey to drink. If he wanted to ever again experience such pleasures, he realized that his only chance at escape was to send his stupid nephew off with both horses.

He sauntered over to Santiago, who had just finished saddling the horses.

"Santiago, you take the horses and go on. Once the pursuers see that two horses have left the valley, they will follow. But not until helping themselves to the meat of the steer. While they feast, I will kill them, then take their horses and catch up with you on the downside of the pass."

Santiago looked at his uncle suspiciously, and thought about the plan for a moment.

"What if they do not stop to feast, Filipio? They will follow the horses quickly, and you will be left here, set afoot."

"They will stop," said Filipio affably. "They, too, have ridden a long, hard trail and will not allow themselves to continue without food.

"It is a perfect trap," he said flatly. Then, summoning a commanding voice, he said, "Now, go. And I will catch up with you at the Sand Mountains. If I am not there in two days, go on to San Luis without me."

Santiago considered the scheme as he continued to

172

pack the saddlebags in the increasing light of dawn. Now, while it was still not yet full light, he realized he had to make a decision fast. He needed to travel, for they were surely being followed. Yet he mistrusted Filipio. He wished desperately for more time to think, yet there was none.

While Santiago thought, Filipio removed his rifle from the sheath connected to the saddle and also removed his bedroll. He picked up a saddlebag in which he had packed cooked meat and offered it to Santiago. The boy warily took it and tied it to his saddle.

Finally, the rising sun made his decision for him. As it shone from beyond the mountains to the east, he jumped astride his horse, tied the reins of Filipio's mount to the back of his saddle, and set off at a walk across the open meadow of the valley.

Behind him, his uncle smiled, waved and spat on the ground. "Goodbye, nephew," he whispered. He snorted softly, then said, "Safe journey."

Sam Tate watched from thirty yards away as the man whose left arm was maimed gazed at the young man riding away. He knew from their descriptions that these were the Garcias, but he was somewhat confused by their actions. Why was the young one, Santiago, leaving?

He had maneuvered himself to the rear of the outlaws' camp nearly an hour before, silently slipping through the thick foliage and constantly moving closer. He carefully carried both of his rifles as well as the handgun. Each was loaded and cocked in preparation for the vengeance that would be his.

His approach resulted from a lifetime of caution. His moccasined feet felt each fallen branch and every rock and silently moved over them. His ears were attuned to the birds, making sure none were spooked into flying across the outlaws' camp. He carefully assessed whether the scent of cooking beef had drawn coyotes in from the hills. And while he did this, his eyes never moved from the two men who were now so near.

When he saw them, his hate was near palpable. It was all he could do not to barge into the camp and kill them then and there. But, as always, caution won out. He wanted to wait for daylight in order to minimize the chance they had of escaping in the darkness. He wanted to be thorough. He wanted this thing to end right here.

Seeing Santiago leading the fatigued horses across the open, grassy valley, Tate felt that he had to move in order to make sure both outlaws were his to claim.

Filipio Garcia seemed on edge and quickly strode to a tree where he had leaned his rifle. He picked it up and checked it, then returned it to its spot before walking a few yards to pick up his gunbelt. Awkwardly attempting to strap the belt around his waist, he cursed as he fumbled with the buckle, unable to fully use his left hand to hold it steady. He finally slipped the belt through the buckle and latched it, then turned back to retrieve the rifle.

A man stood next to it, pointing a huge buffalo rifle directly at Garcia's midsection. Half his body was behind the tree, offering a small target. Dressed in stained buckskins and a low-crowned felt hat, he seemed to be an Indian. Stunned, the outlaw could do nothing but work his jaw back and forth, desperately trying to overcome the shock and regain his senses.

"Seems like yeer pardner's gone and stole yer hosses," said the man flatly, and suddenly Filipio Garcia knew.

Regaining his voice, he said in rough, accented English, "So, it is true. You *are* a ghost."

Tate did not answer, but briefly checked the outlaw over. With a sneer, he said, "Naw, I ain't no ghost. But yee're about to be.

"Yee've hurt me 'n mine. Now, ye die."

"Wait," shouted Garcia, frantically stalling for time. In an

instant, he calculated the distance between his hand and his gun. He knew it wasn't possible, but he had to try something.

"Tate, I didn't know. It was Vivian. He was the one who killed your daughter."

"Makes no nevermind. I 'spect it was ye, though. Yeer brother, he's answering to his God right now. Yee're about to join him."

"Why did you wait, why didn't you shoot before?" asked the frenzied outlaw. "You must have been in the trees. You could have killed me easily from there. Why did you wait?"

"'Cause I wanted ye to look into the eyes 'a hell."

Sam Tate saw the outlaw's arm flash for the pistol. He thought for the briefest instant of letting the hand get there, to somehow give the *bandido* the cruelest of gifts, false hope, but just as quickly rejected the idea. He fired, knocking Filipio Garcia to the ground. The outlaw rolled twice before flopping onto his back, his face turned toward the new day.

The bullet's impact had opened a mortal wound in Garcia's chest, while nearly blowing his right arm from his body. Yet, he continued to breathe as his lifeblood seeped into the soft earth.

The outlaw looked up from the ground at the bright morning sky and was puzzled that he couldn't feel his arm. The pain was excruciating, but was now slipping away. Perhaps the wound was not as bad as he thought. Perhaps...

A shadow passed over his face, and he shifted his eyes toward it. Tate stood over him, his brown face a mask of hate, the rifle slung underneath his left arm. In his right hand, he held a long, grime-encrusted, double-edged knife, newly-honed and gleaming razor-sharp.

The mountain man leaned his face over the outlaw's and whispered, "My rage knows no bounds. It's bigger than this earth and deeper than hell."

175

With bulging eyes, Garcia watched the flashing blade descend in a sweeping arc toward his throat.

Tate slowly stood above the body and tossed the outlaw's head into the center of the clearing. It rolled heavily against a saddlebag, stopping with its horrified eyes seemingly searching the heavens.

The entire exchange had taken only seconds, and the mountain man knew he had no time to contemplate and savor his savage revenge. The younger outlaw had heard the thunder of the buffalo gun and was spurring the horses through the open grass of the valley. As Tate watched, Santiago untied the riderless horse's reins and took off alone. Quickly, Tate retrieved the Henry rifle he'd hidden behind the tree, turned and took aim at the fleeing desperado. The young outlaw was nearly 250 yards across the meadow and moving away as fast as the worn down horse would take him. Tate took a breath and held it, sighting down the long barrel. He slowly squeezed the trigger.

Santiago Garcia was nearing the trees on the far side of the meadow, his mind racing. What had happened? Was Filipio alive? Had they been found? He had attempted to look back to see when he freed the other horse, but the camp was hidden.

Suddenly, he felt as if he had been struck by a hammer in the back. He struggled to stay astride the horse, but saw that the horse was stumbling and going down. He let himself fall from his mount, thudding into the ground just as the report of a shot reached him. As his life ebbed away, he realized it was the delayed sound of the shot that had killed him.

Tate trudged slowly across the meadow, stopping only to skirt small stands of quaking aspen that dotted the grassy valley floor. As he walked, his hate continued to grow. It was unfulfilled, he knew, as hate always was. He could not bring himself to fight it, but embraced it instead.

He approached the crumpled body of the young outlaw

and kicked it over with his foot. The bullet had entered just below the shoulder blade and had exited through the chest. He had been heart shot. Tate then noticed the dead horse. The bullet had passed through the desperado and continued into the horse's neck. That, combined with a heart that had nearly exploded from sheer effort, had killed the animal.

Tate stood in the early morning sun and allowed the emotion to fill him, to run rampant through his body. He screamed aloud at the sky and cursed all the gods of men. Then, he pulled the Spaniard's dagger from his belt again and approached the body of Santiago Garcia.

*"The sack's contents bulged
against the fabric..."*

CHAPTER TWELVE

AMOS HEROLD WAS BESIDE himself with worry. Two hours earlier, he had heard two separate gunshots. The first was Tate's Sharps .50 caliber, its thunderous explosion unmistakable. Then, a minute or so later, another shot echoed through the pristine air, this time from a smaller caliber rifle.

The horses pricked up their ears at the shots, and his father's stallion began pulling on long reins that tied him to a tree. Amos immediately ran to the horse, rubbing and lightly scratching its face to soothe it. In the ensuing silence, the horse calmed down and began nibbling on patches of grass.

The wait since then had seemed interminable, and several times his anxiety threatened to take over. Finally, he began making plans to somehow make his way to the ridge overlooking the valley that Tate had described. Perhaps something could be seen.

Amos picked up the rifle Tate had left him and walked up the grade to the east, figuring he would top out on the ridge. He had gone perhaps only a quarter mile when the forest abruptly opened up as the land fell dramatically away. Stretched out before him was a breathtaking valley with steep forested sides and a grassy meadow bisected by a small, meandering stream. He saw cattle dotting the landscape, and to the far side what seemed to be a dead animal, probably a steer or cow. He squinted his eyes and tried to make it out, then realized the animal was saddled. It had a distinctive blanket tied into a bedroll attached to the saddle. He was staring at a dead horse. Santiago Garcia's dead horse. And nearby was a crumpled mass of clothing that could only be the young outlaw himself.

Fearing that Sam might be in trouble, he decided to quietly make his way down the steep slope toward the dead animal. As he began his descent, he thought he heard someone call. He stopped and listened, remaining completely still. It sounded again and he turned his head. Back above him, framed on the ridgetop, stood Tate.

Amos limped up the slope as fast as his aching body would let him. As he neared the rim, Tate extended his hand and pulled him up.

Out of breath from such exertion at high altitude, Amos was unable to speak for a moment. Finally, his anxiety forced the words from him.

"What happened? I heard shots and then...nothing. I waited, Sam, I waited and waited but I thought you were hurt."

He stopped abruptly as he noticed a dark patch of drying blood on the mountain man's sleeve.

"You're hit? They shot you?" he gasped.

Tate took a long time to speak, and finally let loose a long sigh. Then he said, "Naw, lad. I ain't hit.

"Them divils is dead, lad. They cain't harm nobody ever agin.

"It's over."

Tate turned and strode toward the camp. Amos limped after him, trying to keep up.

"Sam, tell me about it. What happened?

"I, I kept the horses quiet. I thought they were gonna take off and whinny, but I managed to keep 'em quiet."

Tate looked over his shoulder and with a wry, sad smile

said, "That ye did, Amos. An' I'm grateful."

They returned to camp and sat near the picketed horses. Tate looked deeply into the boy's eyes for a moment, then spoke.

"Here's all ye need to know. I found 'em. I kilt the mad dog Filipio, then shot the young 'un as he ran. No more, no less."

Amos was bursting with curiosity, but saw that Tate's mood was deep and dark. Yet, he burned to know what happened. He felt he had a right to know.

"Is that it? Is that all you're going to tell me?" he accused.

Tate stared into the distance, and spoke in a monotone.

"It's never easy to kill a man, son. With mercy on my soul, I swear I've done it afore, but never 'cept as a last resort. I took no pleasure in it, and I want to take no pleasure in it now.

"This is the first time I ever kilt jest fer the killin'," he said quietly.

All was silent except for the birds and the wind. Tate squared his body toward Amos and spoke earnestly.

"Fact is, they's dead, and they won't make nobody else on God's green earth suffer like they made me suffer.

"I've yet to finish this thing, Amos. They's a reward, I understand. I aim to travel on down to Fort Garland and claim it. It belongs to you 'n me 'n Homer."

"But, Sam, I didn't do anything," interrupted the boy.

"You did everythin', lad, everythin'.

"Now, I 'spect Homer 'n his *compadres* to be along shortly, follerin' some sign I managed to leave on the trail. I'm gonna ask Kate 'n Billy to take ye on back to yer folks. I'm sure they need to know about ye, how ye fare.

"I'm gonna ask ye fer a favor, though. I want ye to get word to Esther fer me. Tell her I'm awright, and tell her I've gone to let Kit Carson know there's three less outlaws fer the Army 'a the Missouri to worry 'bout.

"Tell her..." he paused, trying to think of the right words. Then, giving up, he said, "Tell her I'll be home fer good in a coupla days."

Amos nodded, and promised Tate he would deliver the message.

"Thankee, Amos. Now, we need to git the hosses down to that stream fer a drink an' some fine, tall grass. I want ye to foller me, and stay to this side of the valley, hear?"

Amos agreed and followed Tate to the horses. They saddled up and slowly rode over the ridge and down to the river. Spotting the dead horse in the distance once more, Amos asked, "Don't we have to go get their bodies. Pack 'em up and take 'em in for proof?" he asked.

"I awready took care 'a that," Tate answered slowly. "Don't ye worry 'bout it."

They continued on down to the stream, and stayed well away from the valley's far side.

After a couple of hours, they rode the horses back up to their camp, and Tate finally succumbed to exhaustion. He asked Amos to keep a sharp eye out for either friend or foe, then walked into the woods to curl up under some low brush.

It was midafternoon when Amos noticed Lancaster's long ears prick straight up. The horse began pawing the ground and making low noises. Amos turned to call to Tate, but saw the mountain man already standing at the edge of the clearing, looking as if he were carved from the forest's own wood.

Suddenly, a voice sounded down the slope.

"Hail the camp! Ho, the camp! Sam Tate, this here's Homer Keatin', mountain man, hoss soldier, and notorious ladies man. Hero 'a the second battle 'a Adobe Walls and finest riverboat pilot whatever walked dry land. I hail from the Gulf 'o Texas an' I'm callin' yore camp!"

Tate gave a shy smile and yelled back, "C'mon to camp." A minute later, Homer Keating rode into camp, accompanied by the two Ute scouts, Ree and Bobby. Off to the side rode a tall, dark-haired man with a close-cropped beard and a wide-brimmed hat. Next to him rode a short, handsome blond man sporting a sandy-colored moustache. Amos recognized them as Kate Patterson and Billy Carson, General Carson's son.

The men dismounted and stood close to their horses. The Utes stayed apart, quietly talking and gesturing with hand signals while looking at Tate.

Tate and Keating walked toward each other, and Keating reached out to slap Tate on the arm.

"Homer. Billy. Kate." Tate greeted the men in turn.

"How'd ye know 'twas us in this camp? Coulda bin outlaws, ye know."

Keating favored Tate with a sharp stare, then said, "Bobby 'n Ree awready scouted the valley below. Come back with the report of a coupla daid desperados. Least they was thought to be daid desperados. Hard to tell, I heered."

Tate realized that the Utes were talking about him, most likely fearing a man who could conjure up such violence. He answered, "Hard to tell, mebbe, but them jist the same."

Keating grabbed his horse's reins and led it toward the two horses already picketed in the camp. He stopped in front of Tate.

"S'pose this is the best place to camp tonight, afore we do whatever we'll do," he said.

"Yep, s'pose so," answered Tate, his arm sweeping the campsite.

Sometime later, the two Utes came carrying a beef quarter into the camp at Tate's instructions. He reasoned that coyotes would just finish the meat, and that it would be a great waste. After butchering and frying huge slabs of meat, the men settled down and watched the dark overtake the land from the east.

They sat around a small campfire and made plans. Tate

asked his son-in-law Billy all about Mary, how she was holding up. She was now with Esther, so he knew the two women would give each other some measure of comfort.

It was decided that Patterson and Amos would travel east to Francisco's Fort, and from there to Herold's Crossing. Amos would keep Morris's horse for awhile, fattening it up before returning it to Spriggs.

Keating and his scouts would accompany Tate down to Fort Garland. Billy would come along, hoping his father had returned from Taos.

Before turning in, Keating looked at Amos and then good naturedly asked Tate, "How's this here Herold boy holdin' up? He fit to ride the trail with?"

"Yeah, he's fit," answered Tate. "Cept'n he ain't no boy. This 'un here's a man."

The next morning, Amos and Patterson saddled up early after a hasty breakfast of cold beef. Tate stood by Amos's horse and put his hand on the boy's leg. Looking up, he said, "Amos, we'll talk about this more, as we understand it more. Now, go to yer family and give 'em peace.

"Tell yer mam 'n pap that I'll come by soon to 'pologize proper fer bringin' ye on up here with me. I'll also tell 'em I'm glad I did."

The young man smiled down at Tate and stuck out his hand. Tate shook it, and turned to walk away. As he did so, Amos spoke.

"Sam, I had to come. I had to know they were dead. I want you to tell me about it someday—someday before I come back to visit the *conquistadore.*"

Tate nodded his head and looked up at Amos. "That I will, Amos. I promise you that.

"Now, ye just reminded me, lad. Yeer Spaniard's knife."

Tate reached into his buckskin jacket and pulled out the dagger. He'd cleaned away all evidence of its deadly purpose, and now he gingerly held it out to the boy. "Ye done a fine job in honin' 'er up, Amos. A fine job."

Amos accepted the artifact and slipped it into a saddlebag.

Tate backed away as Amos and Patterson rode from camp, heading to the east, toward the *Huajatolla*. Amos turned in the saddle, looked back and waved. Tate responded with the raising of his right arm, his palm to the boy. Staring after Amos, he held his hand in the air longer than was necessary.

After they were gone from sight, Tate looked around the camp and said, "Reckon we best git a leg up, lads."

When the horses were saddled and packed, Tate mounted and rode swiftly into the wall of trees to the south. Not knowing whether to follow, the others stayed behind, finally saddling up. They waited and in a couple of minutes, the mountain man came riding back through.

"Hiyah" he yelled and rode off into the lead. It was only then that Keating noticed the canvas sack tied to the back of Tate's saddle, a sack that had not been there minutes before. The sack's contents bulged against the fabric and bounced up an down against Lancaster's flank in rhythm with the horse's gait.

"...the azure sky framed the purple-blue of the great Spanish Peaks..."

CHAPTER THIRTEEN

THE MIDAFTERNOON SUN was turning the high desert into an oven when Sergeant Ezra Chambers entered Brigadier General Kit Carson's quarters and informed him that five riders were approaching the fort. From the looks of them, it was surely Lieutenant Keating and his scouts, along with two others.

Carson thanked the soldier and dismissed him. He pulled off his stiff cavalry boots and slipped on some well-worn moccasins before slapping his hat on his head and striding out the door. He approached the rampart and asked the soldier on watch for the glass. Looking through it, he saw that the approaching riders were indeed of his company. And riding with them were his son and his closest friend.

Carson had returned from the summit at Taos the day before and was preparing to lead another party over the pass to try to hook up with Tate or Keating. Now, that would seem to be unnecessary.

He ordered the fort's main gate to be opened and walked back to sit in a chair on the porch running in front of his quarters. Over the years, he had learned to wait with dignity, and to face any situation as stoically as possible. Still, he found himself anxiously awaiting the news now being brought to the fort.

The five men rode into the fort, with the two Indian scouts breaking off and heading directly for the corral. Keating, Billy and Tate rode across the dusty parade ground and reined in a few yards from Carson's position. Carson stood and beckoned them from their horses, greeting them effusively. He put his arm around his son's shoulders before returning Keating's salute. He then looked to Tate.

"So, Sam, what news have ye?" he asked, his lined face showing both curiosity and concern.

Tate wearily nodded and reached behind him, untying the knot that secured the canvas bag to the saddle. With an expression of pure wrath, he raised the bag aloft.

"I've news of death and destruction, Kit. Death and destruction."

With a flourish, Tate whipped the bag over his saddle horn and flung it toward the middle of the parade ground. He watched with righteous fury as its contents spilled out in midair before landing with hollow thuds on the hard packed earth.

Kit Carson watched the ghastly severed heads of Filipio and Santiago Garcia roll obscenely for several feet across the parade ground before slowly coming to rest under the blazing high desert sun. He raised one eyebrow in curious expression, then without emotion, he looked back up at his friend.

"Death and destruction, Sam. Yee're right, ye are."

Leaving his son, he stepped off the porch and looked up at Lancaster.

"Thas some fine hossflesh ye've got there, Sam. Light 'n set 'an ye kin tell me how he come to ye. Homer 'n Billy here'll corral him."

Carson looked solemnly at Keating and his son, letting them know that he wished to speak with Tate alone. He opened the door to his quarters, walked inside and pulled out two chairs from around a pine table. As Tate entered, Carson pulled a jug of whisky from an oaken box, then reached into a cabinet and grabbed two glasses. Pouring both full to the brim, he handed one to Tate.

"Sit down, Sam, an' less talk 'bout this."

The absolute fury in Tate's face was undiminished. "Not much to talk 'bout, Kit. I hear they's bounties on they heads. The rest a' they mangy carcasses, *whaugh,* I don't care about."

"I'll hear it all," countered Carson. "Everything ye done since leavin' here."

Tate took a long sip of the whiskey, then sat back heavily in the chair. For the next hour, he told Carson of his return to Francisco's Fort and of tracking the outlaws nearly to the Arkansas Valley before discovering their surprise cutback to Herold's Crossing. He chronicled the kidnapping of Amos Herold and the killing of Vivian Garcia. He described Amos's bravery and the cowardly murder of Wylie Morris. And finally, he told Carson of tracking the murderers, of guessing their whereabouts, of killing them, and of beheading them with the *conquistadore*'s dagger.

Carson listened intently, interrupting occasionally to clarify a point or ask a question. Finally, Tate wound down and the silences between snatches of conversation became long. Carson pursed his lips and gently tugged on his moustache before standing and refilling the glasses.

"That's it then, is it?" he asked quietly.

"I still don't rightly know why the young'un was leavin'. Mebbe they was puttin' together some sorta trap. But they's dead, Kit, and all I know is I done what I done. They'll not kill agin."

Carson nodded in agreement before taking another pull of the sharp whisky. He looked at his friend and saw the hate and confusion imprinted on his face. He knew that throughout his life, Sam Tate never had to face himself in the mirror and see the vision of his hate. Both had known men who had, and they either died from the hate or died from the shame. Carson couldn't bear the thought of either fate for his old *compañero.*

Staring down at the grain of the table before him, Carson said, "Sam, ye're an 'ol hoss. Ain't nothin' I kin say to bring ye the peace ye deserve. But I do know 'bout somethin' else. 'Cause I bin there.

"Naw, we ain't young pups with our lives ahead. We're pretty near groanin' ol' rockin' chair men. Them two heads layin' out there in the dust'll be in pickle jars afore nightfall. By next week, kids'll be paying a penny apiece to some medicine show huckster to take a peek.

"Naw, ye done right, Sam. 'Cept ye started yerself a legend."

Tate gave Carson a quizzical stare. Carson merely nodded and continued.

"Folks back East think I shoot Injuns with one hand while drinkin' whiskey with the other. John Frémont got them silly Eastern writers to make up that foolish stuff. Wanted to make me famous. Well, he did.

"Now, I 'spect they'll soon be talkin' 'bout the mountain man's revenge and the beheadin' of the Garcias. They'll be readin' 'bout Sam Tate in Boston afore the leaves turn.

"They'll come to yer door, Sam. They'll bother ye and they'll bother Esther. And if'n ye shush 'em away like the flies they are, they'll write what they want anyway."

Carson paused to see if Tate was listening. Tate's face was turned toward the window, but Carson could see the attention in his bearing.

"That's what'll happen, Sam. But it's not important.

"Now, I never been long on words," he continued. "Neither've ye. That's suited us both jist fine. But some soul needs to tell ye that what ye done was right. I'll do that now. What ye done *was* right, but now, ye must let it go.

"We both seen men set upon by demons afore. Men who couldn't eat nor sleep. Men who carried they hate on they sleeve. Ever' one 'a them men's molderin' in the ground right now. An' ye need to live."

Tate glanced over at his old companion and saw for the first time, it seemed, the weariness in his face. The toll of being a living legend was steep, indeed. There were responsibilities that were unknown to others who lived in anonymity. But the man whom all America thought of as the absolute essence of the frontier really wanted no more than the friendship and respect of his old companions. "Thankee, Kit," he said. "I'll not be molderin' fer awhile, I 'spect. But I do gotta wonder 'bout things. All my life, I thought things balanced out, somehow. That ye could always find a lesson. It's a hard thing to find," he hesitated. "Well, it ain't true."

Carson smiled and shook his head, nothing more. Presently, he said, "Lemme send word to the Gov'ner. They's a thousand dollars waitin' fer him who kilt the Garcia's."

Tate sighed and squinted while looking out the window.

"Well, it's a thousand to be split three ways, Kit."

"Three ways? You 'n Homer kilt 'em," he said, looking confused.

"Yep, that's true. But young Amos Herold stopped 'em from killin' others, and to my mind, that's better'n shootin' a coupla murderin' thieves."

"Amen," muttered Carson in agreement.

From a desk at the rear of the room he pulled out pen and paper and laid them on the table. He reached to the door and rapped on it, summoning Sergeant Chambers.

Almost immediately, the young soldier opened the door and walked into the room. He stopped and saluted smartly before Carson put him at ease.

"Ezra, this here's Sam Tate, my ol' *compañero.*"

Chambers nodded his head at the grizzled mountain man.

"Afore we start, Ezra, I got a question. Them outlaws' haids still layin' in the dirt yonder?"

"No sir," the young soldier stated. "I believe someone

took them to the infirmary."

"I'll jist bet," chuckled Carson, looking at Tate. Tate let loose a soft snort and sadly shook his head back and forth.

"Well, Ezra," continued Carson, "we got us some official bidness at hand. I want ye to grab that pen and take a letter to th' Gov'ner."

When Chambers was seated with pen in hand, Carson continued.

"Let's try this on fer size. 'Dear Gov'ner, I am pleased to inform ye that the infamous Garcia gang has bin slain. Sam Tate, a man knowed to me for his courage and ability, tracked the murderers through the roughest country of Colorado territory, finally bringin' 'em to bay in a canyon west 'a the Spanish Peaks. The bodies've been positively identified. I request that the reward be forwarded to...'"

Two days later, Sam Tate slowly descended the east side of La Veta Pass and crossed south to the Cucharas River. As he traveled, the magnificent peaks of the *Huajatolla* loomed continually larger. Like a magnet, they drew him home. Home, where Esther now waited for his comfort. Home, where he would no longer hear the laughter of Johnny Gorner. Home, where he planned to teach Amos Herold the secrets of the land.

The past few days had seemed like months, and he found he could not accurately picture his house at the foot of the Spanish Peaks. Like an old friend, its creases and lines were burned in his memory as an entire entity, rather than a juxtaposition of individual parts. Now, he yearned for the friendship of that house as he reflected on the events that had brought him to this stage in his life.

He halted Jake Herold's horse, Lancaster on a rise above the Cucharas River, and looked over the land smoothly spreading out before the *Huajatolla*. Below him lay John Francisco's Fort, which many people were now calling

La Veta. In the distance, the gentle slope of the land fell away in an immense flood plain, densely forested with pinon pine and sage. Above, the azure sky framed the purple-blue of the great Spanish Peaks, its groves of pine and aspen reflecting luminous green. The power of the land itself brought wetness to his eyes.

He whispered into the wind, allowing his voice to be scattered across the landscape.

"Emily, Johnny. We've lost ye, an' I always thought if ye lost somethin, 'ye could find another. Now I find out that somethin's bin lost, awright, but nothin's bin gained."

He sighed heavily, then lightly spurred Lancaster, setting a course that would skirt Fort Francisco and take him home, where he and Esther would face the future together. As the horse descended the broad slope, he whispered once more.

"I s'pose that's life. But it's a hard, hard life."

The Huajatolla listened, and the mountains' spirits were moved.

JON CHANDLER

AUTHOR'S NOTE

The American frontier was, as it has been described, a wild and wooly place. The present day areas of Southern Colorado and Northern New Mexico were part and parcel of the great historical drama that served to weld the continent.

Most of the places described in *The Spanish Peaks* exist, and can be visited today. The town of La Veta is charming, and the Fort Francisco museum at the town's center should not be missed. Fort Garland is a similarly exciting place for those with a passion for the history of the West.

Although *The Spanish Peaks* is fiction, many of its characters are based on historical personalities. Kit Carson, of course, personified the public's image of the frontiersman. Although he is currently undergoing a beating by historical revisionists, he was undoubtedly a first rate mountain man, tracker and guide. Appropriately, his interaction with Indians will long be debated.

John Francisco, Ceran St. Vrain and Albert Boone were also formidable figures in the history of southern Colorado, as was an ancestor of mine, Decatur "Kate" Patterson, who, along with William Green Russell and a group of Georgia miners, discovered gold on the banks of Cherry Creek, giving rise to Denver. He later established La Veta as a colony for Georgians following the Civil War.

The character of Sam Tate is loosely based on the compelling tracker and guide, Tom Tobin. Tobin lived at Fort Garland, on the west side of La Veta Pass, and was indeed one of Kit Carson's close friends (the "me 'n Kit 'et many a beaver tail together" quote is attributed to Tobin), although quite a bit younger than the famed frontiersman. In 1863, Tobin created a Western legend when he took off up La Veta Pass in pursuit of the notorious Espinosa gang, two brothers and a nephew who terrorized the New Mexico/Colorado border. The outlaws were apparently religious fanatics who held a vendetta against Anglo settlers. One had been killed in a battle near Cripple Creek, and Tobin subsequently tracked the other two to La Veta Pass, where he killed them and, out of practicality and perhaps greed rather than revenge, beheaded them. Although Carson commanded Fort Garland before his death in 1868, he was yet to take over that command when Tobin rode in, stopped before Colonel Tappan, and rolled the outlaws' heads at his feet.

It is a historical point of contention as to whether Tobin ever collected the reward—estimated at between $500 and $1,500—for killing the Espinosas.

Some historical juxtaposition was required to develop the plot line of *The Spanish Peaks*. Hopefully, I've managed to capture the flavor and spirit of that time.

Finally, the Spanish Peaks continue to dominate the skyline west of Walsenburg, Colorado. They are a true geologic wonder, reigning over one of the most beautiful areas in the world.

Jon Chandler

ABOUT THE AUTHOR

An accomplished singer, songwriter, and storyteller,
Jon Chandler has released two critically acclaimed
country/Americana recordings, Out West of Laramie and
Keepers of the Flame, winners of nine awards. A director of
the modern-day "Hole in the Wall Gang," Jon lives in Colorado
with his wife, Pat, and their sons. The Spanish Peaks is his
first novel. Other works available by Jon Chandler are:

BOOK

Wyoming Wind
Watch for this exciting new book coming out soon!

COMPACT DISKS

Out West of Laramie
A full-length music CD featuring "The Spanish Peaks," the musical namesake of
the book.

Keepers of the Flame
Another full-length music CD — a tribute to America's farmers and ranchers.

Westerns
Coming soon!

Send order information and inquiries to:
Rodgers & Nelsen Publishing Company
P. O. Box 7001, Loveland, CO 80537-0001
www.RNPub.com   1-970-593-9557

The SPANISH PEAKS

The Western Writers of America, Inc., gives Spur Awards annually for distinguished writing about the American West. These awards are among the oldest and most prestigious in American literature. In 1953, when the awards were established by WWA, western fiction was a staple of American publishing. At the time awards were given to the best western novel, best historical novel, best juvenile, and best short story.

Winners of the Spur Awards in previous years include Larry McMurtry for *Lonesome Dove*, Michael Blake for *Dances With Wolves*, Glendon Swarthout for *The Shootist*, and Tony Hillerman for *Skinwalker*.

Since then the Spur Awards have been broadened to include other types of writing about the West. Today, Spurs are offered for the best western novel (short novel), best novel of the west (long novel), best original paperback novel, best short story, best short nonfiction, best first novel, and others.

The Spanish Peaks by Jon Chandler received the 1999 Spur Award for best first novel.

Western Writers of America was founded in 1953 to promote the literature of the American West and bestow Spur Awards for distinguished writing in the western field. The founders were largely authors who wrote traditional western fiction, but the organization swiftly expanded to include historians and other nonfiction authors, young adult and romance writers, and writers interested in regional history.

OTHER TITLES AVAILABLE FROM
RODGERS & NELSEN PUBLISHING COMPANY

Moods in Wire: A Comprehensive Guide to the Fine Art of Wirewrapping (Volume 1)
by Ellsworth "Ed" Sinclair
ISBN 0-9640483-0-2
$24.95

Moods in Brass & Glass: A Supplementary Guide to the Fine Art of Wirewrapping (Volume 2)
by Ellsworth "Ed" Sinclair
ISBN 0-9640483-1-0
$24.95

Holiday Moods in Wire: An Extended Guide to the Fine Art of Wirewrapping (Volume 3)
by Ellsworth "Ed" Sinclair
ISBN 0-9640483-2-9
$29.95

The Care of Bronze Sculpture
by Patrick V. Kipper
ISBN 0-9647269-1-2
$14.95

Patinas for Silicon Bronze
by Patrick V. Kipper
ISBN 0-9647269-0-4
$69.95

The Successful Writer's Guide to Publishing Magazine Articles
by Eva Shaw
ISBN 0-9662696-1-6
$15.95

Writing the Nonfiction Book
by Eva Shaw
ISBN 0-9662696-2-4
$18.95

Coming soon!
Wyoming Wind
by Jon Chandler

THE SPANISH PEAKS

*Cover Design by Kenn Hayes, Using QuarkXPress for Macintosh,
Title Font—Benguiat Book*

*Text Layout & Electronic Production by Ben Teel using
QuarkXPress for Macintosh, Text Font—ITC Garamond Book*

Original Pen & Ink Illustrations by Beverly J. Nelsen

Cover Photo of the Spanish Peaks by Gordon Kelley Photography

Text Editing by Barbara Teel

Cover Stock is 12 Point Coated One Side White with Film Laminate Coating

Text Stock is 55# Vellum, Offset in "Natural" Color

Printed and Perfect Bound by United Graphics Incorporated